Three colleagues—three reasons to doubt
Three couples who must put the past behind them. . .for love

'A year apart would make an easy preliminary to divorce,' Helen said.

There! After all her resolve, she had still been the first one to mention the word that lately had been drumming with such an ugly rhythm in her head.

She heard his hissing intake of breath. They were still holding each other, clutching each other stiffly now, and it held no comfort. All it did was help her read more clearly the signals coming from his familiar body. This tightness in every muscle, this iron control in him.

Was it guilt? An attempt to conceal relief?

Dear Reader

My starting point was the relationship between Nick and Helen in FULL RECOVERY. Thinking about their happy marriage, I started to wonder, What will come afterwards? Inevitably, circumstances change and there are challenges. As I wrote, I became intrigued by the characters of Megan and Karen and wanted to know what would come afterwards for them, too. In FULL RECOVERY Karen is swept off her feet by the wrong man. How does this affect her happiness later on with the right one? A GIFT FOR HEALING answers the question. And what about Megan? We know her in FULL RECOVERY as the Other Woman, but is it fair to dismiss her that way? Doesn't she deserve the right man too? I had to find him for her and then wrote MISLEADING SYMPTOMS to bring them together. All in all, I felt as much page-turning curiosity as any reader as this trilogy unfolded.

Lilian Darcy

FULL RECOVERY is the first book of Lilian Darcy's Camberton Hospital trilogy. Look out for Karen in A GIFT FOR HEALING in April 1997, and Megan in MISLEADING SYMPTOMS in May 1997.

FULL RECOVERY

BY
LILIAN DARCY

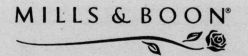

MILLS & BOON®

*First published in Great Britain 1997
Harlequin Mills & Boon Limited,
Eton House, 18-24 Paradise Road, Richmond, Surrey TW9 1SR*

© Lilian Darcy 1997

ISBN 0 263 80051 2

*Set in Times 10 on 11 pt. by
Rowland Phototypesetting Limited
Bury St Edmunds, Suffolk*

03-9703-54210-D

*Printed and bound in Great Britain
by Mackays of Chatham PLC, Chatham*

CHAPTER ONE

'WELL, the house certainly seems empty without them,' Dr Nick Darnell observed to his wife, his voice emerging from behind the fridge door.

'What brought that on?' Helen Darnell laughed, not looking at him. She was busy heaping coffee into the conical paper filter at the top of the coffee-maker, its aroma rousing senses that were still of the opinion that bed was worth far more than breakfast. 'You've had your head stuck in the fridge ever since I came in.'

'Yes,' Nick grumbled. 'In a relentless quest, and thus far a fruitless one, for the yoghurt. I could always be fairly certain of finding it somewhere behind Jon's ghastly fizzy drinks or Jane's home-made avocado, oatmeal and Marmite face-cream.'

'Honey, my love.'

'What, next to the honey? No. . .'

'No, Jane's face-cream. Honey, not Marmite.'

'Whatever. It was almost always there. Now, with the face-cream and the fizzies off to London, the fridge is so empty that I can't find a thing!'

'Try in the door section, next to the juice.'

'Aha! Exceptional woman! Now, if you could only solve this problem of the mysterious green spot on my shirt cuff. . .'

But Helen fled in the direction of the shower, pretending not to hear this last part. Six-thirty in the morning was really *too* early to have to think about shirt-cuff stains!

Nick watched her go, wishing he had managed a quick squeeze before her departure. She wasn't a 'morning person' but that somehow did nothing to lessen her attractiveness to him at this hour. With her chestnut-red hair standing out like a bush and her full breasts and rounded bottom softly emphasised by the fuzzy fabric of her dark blue dressing-gown, she probably had no idea how much she enticed him. For a moment he felt a spurt of very selfish pleasure at the fact that they were essentially alone now, followed by a twinge of guilt.

It was going to be hard for Helen. She had always been such a generously giving wife and mother. He wondered if she even knew how to take care of her own needs. They had married so young—twenty years ago today—and, not for the first time, he wondered, Should I have insisted that we wait? He had been in as much of a hurry as she had but, at three and a half years her senior, should he have been more responsible and counselled caution in the face of her starry-eyed impatience?

He still considered that most of the sacrifices had been hers over the years, and the thought that she might have had more choices—more freedom—if he had made them wait was a guilty secret that he didn't dare to share with her in case. . .

What? He looked his fear in the face in an attempt to understand it, his earlier spurt of pleasure quite gone now. With more time, what might Helen discover about her needs? Something that threatened the very foundation of their lives together? It wouldn't be the first time that an empty nest revealed unexpected emptiness in a marriage as well.

Listening to the sound of the water running, he muttered aloud, 'If only the timing of everything this month wasn't so terrible. . .'

In the shower, Helen was thinking that Nick had been quite right. The house *did* seem empty without the twins, delivered to London and their new university digs just last Friday. We're rattling around like dried beans in a pod, she thought as she showered. And I don't know if I want to be in floods of tears about it, or start celebrating the fact that we've got time to ourselves at last.

Not all that much time to themselves, actually, she revised. Nick was even more frantic than usual at the hospital today and at her own work, after she and Nick made their harried departure from the house, Helen had to make a dozen delicate phone calls, as well as running her single mothers' group which went from ten until twelve.

This led inevitably to a lunch of sandwiches and a cup of tea at her desk, with the consequent threat of marking her reports with rings of moisture from the bottom of the mug. . .

'Working through your lunch-break again, Helen?' drawled Stella Harris, entering the crowded open-plan office at half past twelve.

This was the nerve-centre for the community nursing component of the busy health centre in the small Midlands city of Camberton, and there was rarely a moment during the day when it was completely quiet. There were three of them in here now and, across the corridor, the four GPs in the practice were having a lunchtime meeting.

'Well, it's better than having to stay late,' Helen answered her colleague wryly. 'Although I'd really have to do that as well if I was going to make any sort of decent dent in this paperwork. At least my mileage log is up to date.'

'So's mine,' announced Marcella McPherson, the most junior of the practice's community nursing staff, dropping her pen triumphantly onto the desk. 'And everything else can wait because tonight is one night I'm *not* staying late. It's Alan's and my first wedding anniversary!'

'Oh, congratulations!' said Anne Robson, one of the district nurses, who had entered in time to hear the announcement. 'Got something special planned, I hope?'

'Of course,' Marcella grinned, 'and some of it's *not* fit for public consumption!'

'You mean what was in that pink bag from the lingerie boutique you turned up with after lunch yesterday?' Anne teased.

This time Marcella had the grace to blush. 'Well, if I can't wear a sexy nightie for my hubby, what's the world coming to? But, knowing him,' she said lovingly, 'he'll only notice the food.'

'You're not going out?'

'No, I wanted to cook him something wonderful, since it's beans on toast or frozen pies most other nights. I've been slaving in that kitchen for days!' She outlined an ambitious menu, and then stopped as Helen came in with a blurted exclamation of dismay.

'What's the matter, Helen?' Stella asked, and all three women looked at her.

She felt foolish. 'Oh, it's nothing. It's just that. . . Well, actually, it's my wedding anniversary today, too, and I was planning to cook, and I've just remembered I don't have a single green vegetable in the house—not even a lettuce.' The realisation gave new meaning to Nick's observation about the emptiness of the fridge this morning.

'Your wedding anniversary? Really? The twelfth?' Marcella had turned to her with shining eyes. 'Isn't that a coincidence? I always think it's such a nice date, too, don't you? September the twelfth! How many years have you been married?'

'Well, you may not believe it—I hardly believe it myself when I think about it—but it's twenty!'

'Twenty!' Marcella was aghast.

'Incredible, isn't it? But, after all, the twins are eighteen.'

'And you're not going away to Paris for the weekend, or something?'

'Paris! No! In fact, Nick's off to a conference in Boston tomorrow, by himself.' Which she was *not* looking forward to!

'But you *are* doing something romantic, aren't you?' Marcella beseeched her.

'I hadn't really planned anything, other than dinner,' Helen admitted, and then, with all eyes upon her and feeling very self-conscious and uncomfortable, she tried to sound flip and funny. 'When you've been married as long as we have, there's not a lot of romance left in it!'

The humour didn't come off. Marcella looked shocked and disappointed, and the light had gone from her eyes. Helen grew hot with remorse. Her comment had sounded horribly disloyal to Nick, whom they all knew, but it was too late to withdraw it now and she knew that she had left her co-workers with the impression of a tired, staid union, kept going by convenience and convention alone. That couldn't be true, could it? She and Nick— in an empty marriage?

She remembered once again how empty the house had felt this morning, and how preoccupied Nick had seemed when she returned from the shower. He'd been hunched over his coffee, and staring into it with a frown and a narrowed gaze that he didn't bother to explain. The conference, she had thought at the time, and hadn't pestered him. Now she wondered if it was more than that.

'For heaven's sake, Helen!' Stella was saying. 'If that's the case, why don't you have an affair?'

'Stella!'

'No, don't look so open-mouthed and innocent about it. If your marriage is jogging along like a tired old horse, it's the obvious thing to do.'

'But it's not just an issue of—Stella, you're making it sound like someone taking a tonic if they're feeling a bit run-down.' And my marriage *isn't* run-down, she wanted to insist, but it would sound hollow after that *stupid* comment about lack of romance. Why on earth had she said it? The fact that she was suddenly wondering if there could be a grain of truth in the idea only made the thing worse.

'Well, why not look at it that way and *take* the tonic?' Stella was demanding now. 'I wish it's what I'd done— got in a bit of delicious infidelity so that at least I'd have been left with something to gloat over!'

Her laughter was a harsh bark, and everyone looked sympathetic and uncomfortable. The oldest member of the community nursing team, Stella Harris had returned to the workforce a year ago after a bitter and painful divorce. Her husband, Raymond, had left her after twenty-five years of marriage to live with a twenty-year-old secretary, who was now his second wife. The rejection, coupled with its consequent loss of status and security, had devastated Stella and left her with a hard shell of bitterness that seemed to be her only way of making sense of what had happened.

Now Helen found herself wondering, Could Nick ever do something like that? A forceful *no* was her immediate answer to this question. Nick was utterly loyal and straight. It was one of the countless things that she had always loved about him.

So why wouldn't the niggling doubt go away? She definitely felt unsettled at the moment, churned up and more emotional than usual. Jane's face-cream gone from the fridge; Jon's CD collection leaving a big hole in the rack below their stereo equipment; Nick with nothing to say to her at breakfast. . .

Stella was still talking about the therapeutic benefits of infidelity. 'Seriously, Helen.' Her voice had dropped now, and the others were getting cups of tea and opening their diaries ready for the two case conferences about to take place. Dr Anderson would be joining them, as well as Linda Marshall, a nurse from nearby Camberton Hospital's palliative care team. 'If an affair is what you need to pep up your marriage—or your life—just do it! Don't hang back out of any silly qualms about your marriage vows. When it comes to the crunch, they mean nothing to a man. Less than nothing! Why should we let it be different for us?'

'Stella, I have no desire whatsoever to have an affair!' Helen said helplessly. 'And I'm sure Nick doesn't either. When I talked about lack of romance just now I was joking. It was silly, and I shouldn't have said it. It's... it's not true, actually, and Nick would never—'

'"Nick would never",' Stella mimicked bitterly. 'Raymond would never; Matthew, Mark, Luke and John would never. There are women all over the country using exactly those words and, meanwhile, Tom, Dick and Harry—or Tom, *Nick* and Harry—are busily ogling anything in skirts.'

'Well, perhaps just a bit of ogling,' Helen laughed, secure in the conviction that Nick didn't even do that. For one thing, his work as a consultant thoracic physician at nearby Camberton Hospital kept him far too busy!

'So why shouldn't you do some ogling of your own?'

'Not sure that I'd still know how,' she answered lightly, although that wasn't the point. 'I was only seventeen when Nick and I were married.'

'My God, you were a baby! Young, I knew, but seventeen? And you haven't looked at another man since? Helen, honestly, you absolutely owe it to yourself to at least ogle! In fact, I've even got someone in mind. My new next-door neighbour-but-one. He was in here this morning to see Dr Snaith. You didn't notice—?'

'No, I didn't, but thanks for the tip!' She gave a light laugh, then added very firmly, '*Not* that I intend to act on it!' Stella seemed to get the message at last and the subject was dropped, much to Helen's relief.

Linda Marshall had arrived now, in any case, and Dr Anderson wanted to know if he had time to grab a tea... The case conferences were about to begin, and Helen wasn't sorry.

An innocent, if ill-conceived remark had led to a far more serious and disturbing discussion with Stella than she ever would have wanted and, what was worse, she knew that she had left all three women with an awful impression of her marriage. She couldn't get this out of her mind... *Was* there anything wrong between herself and Nick? And knew when the case conferences were finished that she hadn't focused on the issues at hand as she should have done.

Taking her small health service car to drive up to the hospital to visit some patients came as a relief—the chance to be alone—and she took the opportunity to dash quickly into the local greengrocer for some out-of-season asparagus and an exotic variety of lettuce. She and Nick would at least have a nice meal tonight, and perhaps that would get rid of this troubling idea that her well-seasoned marriage might not be immune to problems.

Had she and Nick been resting on their laurels? Had the presence of the twins camouflaged an unacknowledged rift?

No! I'd have felt it, wouldn't I? I would!

She plunged into the busy, familiar world of Camberton Hospital, feeling somewhat better, and managed to push the subject from her mind as she caught up with the two mothers on her list. One was just a social visit, really, to Jenny Pettit, who had given birth for the third time yesterday—to twins. The eldest was still on Helen's case list of under-fives, and she was a little worried that four children under the age of four would prove too much for this conscientious but hot-tempered mother.

Helen had already noted, for example, that the two-year-old was behind with her immunisations, and Mrs Pettit had reported that Andrew, three and a half, had lost ground with his toilet training and she was 'at her wit's end' with him about the 'accidents' that occurred almost daily. There was no harm, therefore, in paying a friendly, supportive call here in hospital before the officially scheduled visit to Mrs Pettit's home when the twins were ten days old.

She found Jenny tired but cheerfully determined to squeeze every minute of rest that she could from this hospital stay. 'Mum's at home with Andrew and Grace,' she said, 'and I've wangled two extra days in here. Bliss!' She stretched back against the pillows and smiled.

'Don't forget to eat as well as sleep,' Helen said.

'You don't have to tell me that!' Mrs Pettit had breast-fed both Andrew and Grace, and wanted to do the same with the twins.

'I breast-fed my twins,' Helen told her, 'so if you need any extra pointers. . .although I may have forgotten everything I ever knew by this time!'

'Really? But they can't be that old, yours, can they? Ten? Twelve?'

'Try eighteen,' Helen supplied with a laugh.

'No! You're not old enough!' Flattering, of course, and just what she needed on a day that hadn't done much for her confidence so far.

Remembering clues in the Pettits' kitchen which suggested that meals were fairly ad hoc, Helen made a note in her diary after she had left the maternity ward to have a brain-storming session with Jenny once she was home about ways to ensure better-planned meals and easy-access but nutritious snacks for the whole family.

Her next mum and baby, Freda Minty and ten-day old Rebecca, were across in Neonatal Intensive Care, and she was visiting them here because it would still be some time before Rebecca, almost twelve weeks premature, was able to go home. That in itself was a very stressful situation for both parents, and she had already talked by phone with NICU ward sister, Monica Doughty, about Freda Minty's post-partum blues.

Monica met her on the ward as she came in and said with a grimace, 'Bad timing, Helen. She needs to be seen, but she's just gone off to sleep in the parents' stay-over room and Roger Thompson, who was on last night, told me she'd been sitting with Rebecca constantly from eleven last night right through till morning. She's exhausted, and I *really* don't want to wake her.'

'No, of course not,' Helen agreed. 'Is she spending any time at home at all?'

'No. She went home to shower yesterday morning, but that's it. I'm glad she's involved and connected to the baby, but she's going to wear herself out.'

'I'll ask Dr Anderson if he has any ideas. Mrs Minty's mother is a patient of his, too. Perhaps Mrs Minty would accept her sitting with Rebecca sometimes.'

'I think possibly she would,' Monica nodded, 'but I gather there's a transport problem.'

'That's right, Mrs Shaw had polio and doesn't walk too well. I wonder if there's a handicapped-access mini-bus that could add her to their route on pre-arranged days.' Helen made another note in her diary. 'I'll try and catch Mrs Minty tomorrow, then.'

'A morning visit might work better,' Sister Doughty suggested.

'Meanwhile, can I have a look at the babe?'

'Surely!'

Rebecca was tiny, and terrifyingly dependent on tubes and needles. She weighed only just over two pounds but was 'a real fighter', according to Sister Doughty. Still, there were problems ahead and the Minty family would have special needs during Rebecca's protracted hospital stay, and once she was safely home as well.

The last patient on Helen's hospital list this afternoon was Agatha Miller, an elderly woman with chronic bronchitis and emphysema, and as she crossed the open courtyard that provided a short cut from the maternity wing to the main building she was thinking of the fact that this was one of Nick's patients and that she might see him.

The possibility did strange things to her insides, after

his frowning silence this morning—coupled with what Stella had said to her over lunch—and she wanted to see him very badly. Surely it would only take one quick word or two between them to reassure herself that everything was fine!

Helen was well known on the chest ward, of course. Nick Darnell had been one of the consultant thoracic physicians at Camberton Hospital for almost five years now, and she occasionally had patients on her own case list to see here—as she did today. Ward Sister Gloria Edmondson greeted her at the nurses' station.

'I don't think Dr Darnell is with us at the moment, Mrs Darnell. . . Or are you here to see a patient?'

'Agatha Miller,' Helen confirmed, trying to sound as businesslike as possible. Nick wasn't here. Damn. . .

'Bed Fourteen,' Gloria told her. 'Her daughter wants to have her once she's discharged. Is that why you're here?'

'Yes. I'll be visiting the daughter, Barbara James, at home tomorrow. She's very keen, apparently.'

Gloria made a face. 'Hmm. . .' And then, in a lowered tone, 'She can be difficult, our Agatha, and a bit confused at times. I hope Mrs James knows what's involved. She has young children at home, apparently.'

'Yes. Have they visited her in here, do you know?'

'No, I don't think so.'

'It might be a good idea if they did, to get used to how she looks, as some of the respiratory equipment might be going home with her, mightn't it?'

'Yes, at first, certainly, and very possibly on an ongoing basis. This was a major respiratory failure. She'll need oxygen.'

'Lots to think and talk about, then.'

'If Dr Darnell does come in, shall I tell him you're here?'

'Only if he's not too busy,' Helen said stoutly, determined to be sensible. After all, she had lived with the man for twenty years and would see him tonight at dinner.

She *should* be thinking purely about the patient she was
about to assess.

Bed Fourteen. The chest ward had been extended
recently, and all the numbers had been changed. One
long Nightingale ward was now eight two-bed rooms, and
there were four private rooms as well down a different
corridor. She tried the corridor first, going past two temporarily empty rooms, and then heard an elderly woman's
voice right at the end. Aha!

She poked her head through the open door, then
realised that this was Bed Twelve. There was someone
with the patient—a doctor with a white coat flung onto
the back of the chair behind him, and a stethoscope
around the smooth neck that was revealed by a fresh
haircut.

The well-shaped head was partially silhouetted against
the light from the window, as was a lean but capable
body in a soft olive-green shirt with a subtle geometric
pattern scattered across it. He moved slightly, and the
sinew and muscles in his shoulders played beneath the
draped contours of the shirt. An attractive physique. . .

But since this wasn't her patient after all Helen took
in the scene in just a second or two and withdrew again,
suddenly thinking of Stella's disturbing suggestion after
lunch that she should have an affair—or at least ogle
a little.

Perhaps she'd consider that chap ogling material,
Helen smiled to herself and then, as if to punctuate the
thought, she heard the doctor laugh in the room
behind her.

'You certainly know your own mind, Mrs Gordon!'

And only then did she realise that it was Nick.

It came as quite a shock, and left her breathless and
burning. He's had his hair cut over lunch. It makes his
head look so nice! And he must have bought that shirt,
too. That's right, he was a bit peeved this morning about
the stain on the cuff of the one he was wearing and all

his other good ones were in the wash, ready for Boston tomorrow. My God, I almost took Stella's advice, and the man I was planning to ogle was my own husband!

Coming after that awful conversation at lunch, and the nagging, uncomfortable doubts she had felt, the trick her eyes had played on her was horribly disturbing. If Gloria Edmondson had not told her—mistakenly, it was now clear—that he wasn't on the ward at the moment then, of course, she would have recognised him at once. The fact that she *hadn't*. . .

He'll laugh about it when I tell him!

But, no, it wasn't just an amusing anecdote to be relayed over dinner. Helen's heart was still hammering, and she knew she wasn't at all ready to seek out her patient yet. What on earth was wrong with her? She didn't want an affair! And she didn't need to feel so churned up over Nick! Taking temporary refuge in a bathroom on the opposite side of the ward, she saw hectic cheeks and wild eyes that looked stormily green against her rich chestnut hair. 'I'm like a teenager with a crush, but this is my husband!'

Splashing water on her face to cool it and then patting her fiery cheeks dry, Helen made to leave the bathroom again. Time was getting on. But when she opened the door it was to see Megan Stone, Nick's senior registrar, standing in the corridor some distance off, just outside Bed Twelve.

She was straightening her pencil-slim skirt and tailored silk blouse in an oddly tentative, nervous way, and running a quick comb through her healthy sweep of ash-blonde hair. Seconds later she disappeared into the patient's room, and once more Helen was considerably rattled.

She had always been very fond of Megan, and had worried about her at times, too. A stunningly attractive thirty-two-year-old and a very intelligent and caring doctor, Megan had an odd streak of self-doubt threaded through her inner make-up. Was that why she was still single? Helen had wondered more than once. Or was it *because* she was still single?

Once she had tried to pair Megan up with Dr Snaith in the health centre practice but Megan had seemed nervous and rather brittle during the small dinner party; the two of them hadn't clicked, and Helen hadn't tried it again. Perhaps the ambitious senior registrar just wasn't interested in a relationship, was her conclusion.

Now, though. . . Megan *hadn't* been tidying herself up like that just to impress an elderly woman with chronic bronchitis!

Still standing weak-kneed just outside the bathroom door, Helen saw Nick and Megan come out of the patient's room, deep in conversation. Megan was pointing something out to him in the notes she carried, leaning close enough that her hair swung against his jaw, and from this distance it almost looked as if their fingers could be touching. Then she stepped back a bit and looked up at the tall man at her side, her lashes long, her gaze. . .*adoring*?

And it was suddenly as if Helen was really *seeing* her husband for the first time.

He had been eighteen when they met and twenty when they'd married, with all the earnestness and uncertainty of a struggling medical student—as well as a medical student's occasional need to break out and do something totally idiotic. She had been Helen Patterson back then and, at fifteen, he was her first boyfriend. Her only boyfriend. Her schoolfriends had kindly told her that he was 'very dishy' and she had been so in love that she would have been outraged if anyone had suggested that he was anything other than physical perfection.

But, in fact, he had been nothing special, still youthfully skinny and so smooth-faced that shaving was just a joke. The long hair that was then the fashion had been brushed down in a thick fringe almost covering his eyes, giving him a rather Neanderthal air, and after late nights of study, the occasional adolescent blemish had made its appearance on his skin.

Now, though. . . His figure had filled out so that, although still without an ounce of superfluous fat, it was tautly muscled and strong. Frequent walking and summer tennis kept him athletic and fit, too. His skin had cleared up long ago and fashions in hair had changed vastly for the better. The earnestness and uncertainty had grown gradually into a professional confidence and personal maturity that gave him a relaxed, yet dignified and upright bearing, a compassionate manner and a wickedly dry sense of humour.

Incredibly, Nick was forty now. There were some silver threads sprinkled at his temples and some lines etched into his intelligent face but, in a man, these things only served to emphasise the fact that he was in his prime and had added nuances of depth and experience to his nature. His grey eyes were still clear and fringed with dark lashes; his voice was still strong and deep and vibrant; his male sensuality was still a potent yet well-schooled force—and it would be many years yet before these attributes began to fade.

For the first time Helen was alive to the realisation that her husband was an incredibly attractive man, and in the same moment she had discovered that she was not the only woman to think so. Not by any means!

She ducked quickly back into the bathroom as Nick and Megan wandered towards her along the corridor, still wrapped in a discussion that she told herself *had* to be professional. . .although, from the way the blonde senior registrar was lifting her strong, pretty chin and tossing her smoothly coifed hair, it needn't have been.

'Megan's in love with him,' she whispered faintly. 'Why didn't I see it before? How long has she felt that way?'

And, if it hadn't been for that discussion with bitter

Stella after lunch, she might have dismissed the knowledge with an indulgent laugh. Now, her knees were weak and she had to fight to pull herself together.

So Megan had a crush. It meant nothing. Nick couldn't possibly return it. Doubtless he wasn't even aware of it.

'Perhaps I should say something about it to him. . .' He might be gently amused.

But, no, because if he hadn't realised how Megan felt she didn't want to put ideas into his head.

Just what kind of ideas Helen didn't let herself be too specific about, and a minute later she forced herself to leave the bathroom, intending to go up to Nick and Megan and damp down these ridiculous, nonsensical fears with a bit of small talk. Surely she would see at once that she had been imagining things. Nick would touch her in some quick, casually intimate way—at the thought of this, her skin tingled—and everything would suddenly be all right.

When she emerged, however, Nick seemed to have gone and Megan, catching sight of her, confirmed this.

'If you were looking for Nick, Helen, then you've just this minute missed him, I'm afraid.' Although she seemed genuinely concerned, Helen suddenly found that she distrusted those neatly frowning brows.

'That's all right,' she told her husband's senior registrar steadily. 'I'll see him tonight. I'm really here to visit a patient.'

'Mrs Gordon? We've just—'

'No, Mrs Miller. Bed Fourteen.'

'I'll come with you,' Megan offered. 'I know she's having a difficult time.'

Helen tried to overlook her own reluctance. Megan had a perfect right to visit her patients, and it might even help to establish the rapport she needed to find with the elderly woman. 'Good, because I haven't caught up with you for a while, Megan,' she said brightly. 'This will give us the chance for a chat.'

'Yes, because you're not coming with Nick tomorrow, are you?' Megan said as they turned down the new corridor that had once been one side of the old Nightingale ward.

'To Boston? No, it wasn't very well timed for me,' Helen answered. And only now did she remember that Megan herself was going to the conference too. 'We talked about it, but—'

'Excuse me?' A frail elderly man was coming towards them. He had looked at Megan but was, perhaps, intimidated by her slim height and white coat because now he turned to Helen, who wasn't in uniform, and laid a slightly shaky hand on her arm. 'I'm looking for Bed Twelve, but it's missing.' He stopped, coughed, wheezed and began again. 'There are numbers one to eight, and thirteen to twenty-one, but the middle ones are missing.'

'I know,' Helen said with a smile. 'They've done it in a silly way, haven't they? Nine, ten, eleven and twelve are all down the other corridor.'

'Past where the nurses sit?'

'That's right.'

'Thank you, missy.' He patted her and shuffled off.

'I'm looking forward to the conference immensely,' Megan began again as soon as the elderly man had taken a step or two away from them. 'And so is Nick. . . As I—I'm sure you know,' she added quickly.

'Oh, yes,' Helen agreed.

The name on Megan's lips had sounded a little possessive, but Helen was actually thinking more about the elderly man. Mr Gordon, evidently, if he was going to visit his wife in Bed Twelve. Was he also a chronic bronchitis sufferer? It seemed likely. There really ought to be a support and education group for people such as the Gordons. She had thought this before, then allowed herself to be frightened off by the amount of extra work involved in organising and running such a thing.

This made her feel bad now. With the twins gone, she

would have more time and she really ought to do it. Nick could give her a list of likely candidates, as could the doctors in the group practice where she was based. That would be a good start, and then word could be spread through a variety of channels. . .

But Megan was still talking about Boston, and they hadn't made any further progress towards Bed Fourteen at the far end of the corridor. Helen hadn't fully been listening, and still wasn't as she plotted the support group in her mind.

'This other possibility. . .' she vaguely heard. 'Wonderful if it comes off. . . Ready for a change of scene for a year or so. . .' Limit it to chronic bronchitis and emphysema sufferers? There were a number of people with occupational lung diseases in the area, but it would lose its usefulness if it became too big. 'And I've heard Boston is a lovely city.'

Helen refocused guiltily. 'Boston a lovely city? Yes, apparently. It would be nice to go, but university starts next week and the twins are in their first year. I want to be in the country, at least, in case they need me. And then there's the cat!'

'The cat? Pushcart?' Megan laughed. 'Love the name. . .'

'Oh, Nick called her that—he didn't intend to, but it stuck—after a toy Jonathon loved at the time. He couldn't say the difference between ''Puss-cat'' and ''pushcart'', you see. The twins were only two when we got her.'

'Nick really is just priceless!' Megan exclaimed warmly, and Helen was irritated. It wasn't all *that* funny!

She went on, 'Anyway, seriously, it would be expensive for me to go over for something like that.' She was thinking of the luxury hotel where the conference was being held. Just her meals alone would probably cost the earth. 'And Nick's bound to be embroiled in his work so much of the time, it's not as if we'd be able to do much together.'

'True,' Megan agreed. Then she added hesitantly, 'You're very practical about it all, aren't you?'

The question was innocent but Helen bristled inwardly all the same.

'It's only for six days,' she answered, far too tartly.

'Six days?' Megan looked alarmed. 'Oh, heavens, I was talking about this possibility of going over for a year!'

'Oh, in that case—'

'But, after all, you're right, the same considerations still apply, don't they?' Megan swept on at a bit of a gabble, frowning. 'Your job, the twins. I can understand that you might decide in favour of staying behind. And I imagine one feels differently after being married for a while. Nick mentioned it was your wedding anniversary today, but he didn't say how long since you'd actually done the deed.' She chuckled.

'Twenty years,' Helen supplied, then added—not too pointedly, she hoped, 'Twenty wonderful years. And, really, this year in Boston, I have no intention of—'

'Twenty? My goodness! But, of course, the twins are over nineteen now, aren't they?'

'Eighteen,' Helen corrected firmly, distracted now.

Had Megan been implying what so many people wrongly assumed? That she and Nick had got married because the twins were already on their way? Mostly she didn't mind if casual acquaintances thought this. Let them, if their minds worked that way! But somehow she wanted Megan Stone to be quite clear that the dates added up as they should.

'That's quite an achievement, then, Helen,' Nick's senior registrar was saying sincerely. 'Twenty years. Congratulations! It's quite rare, I think, for such a youthful marriage to last so long. People often go through such big changes in their twenties that a marriage can't survive. Or if it does, it's just an empty shell...as it's always been for my parents. I often wish one of them had met someone else—to give them the impetus to end the farce. That's all it can take, I think...meeting someone else...' Her blue eyes were focused on some abstraction in the air. 'But if you and Nick really are still going strong...that's a real achievement.'

This last bit was very bright, too enthusiastic to be quite sincere, and Helen suddenly wondered, Is she lonely? Is that why she's hinting so broadly that our marriage is empty? Does this mean she thinks my husband is fair game?

This was the definite impression she got from what Megan had said. Not just the words, but the smile and the tone and the body language—the softening of Megan's crisp consonants as she said Nick's name, the frowning glance that assessed Helen's mature figure and the slight nodding of her head as she expressed her considered opinion that most youthful marriages would be better off dead.

Perhaps Megan's biological clock was beginning to tick, Helen thought, trying to summon some empathy for someone she had always liked. Today she didn't succeed.

If she could get him, she'd have no qualms about taking him. She's already rationalised the whole thing to herself with that idea about youthful marriages, Helen decided angrily. She probably wouldn't feel that she was doing anything wrong at all.

A bleeper sounded from the breast pocket of Megan's coat at that moment. 'Oh, dear, that'll be my new cystic fibrosis baby over on Neonatal.' She looked concerned, and her face softened and fell into different lines with the new emotion. 'I must go. He's such a dear little bloke and the parents are distraught. I told Sister Doughty to page me as soon as they were ready to talk. I'll have to come back and see Mrs Miller later.'

She clicked away towards the lift in her smart red high

heels and Helen, who felt dowdy now in the flat white sandals she had worn today, just had time to call after her, 'Enjoy the Boston conference!' before Megan disappeared. Hearing the insincerity in her own voice, she wondered, am I just being a suspicious old cow? God, I feel like one! I certainly feel *old*!

But the whole conversation had definitely left a sour taste. It was like a jungle encounter in which a junior lioness had suddenly turned on the queen of the pride and, though it seemed ridiculous, Helen was left with the distinct impression that a covert battle had been enjoined and that she was in competition with Megan Stone for her own husband.

CHAPTER TWO

'WHAT do you think of this oxygen equipment, Mrs Miller?' Helen joked. 'It's not much to look at, is it?'

'I'll have my portable for when I need to get about,' Agatha Miller wheezed.

'Yes, that's a blessing, isn't it? But you must be careful not to get into the habit of relying on the portable because the oxygen in that runs out fairly quickly and has to be replaced. Use the tank whenever you're sitting down.'

'It's all right, love, I'm used to the oxygen.' Agatha patted Helen's hand reassuringly. 'I had it before at home—when I was at my own place. I didn't always bother with the nose-tube thing or the whatchamacall it. . .Ventimask. I didn't like those so much. If I just held the hose up near my face and took little whiffs it did the trick just as well.'

'I see,' Helen said. 'That was your own idea, was it?'

'Oh, yes, the doctors don't tell you those things. All they ever say is to stop smoking, as if that's going to do me any good now!'

A little concerned, Helen made a mental note. She would have to mention this matter of the oxygen to Mrs Miller's daughter, Barbara James, and to Anne Robson who would be making visits in her capacity as district nurse. Patients often tended to use oxygen inappropriately, treating it like a vague sort of tonic—as benign and harmless as a breath of fresh air. But there were dangers. For one thing, oxygen was combustible and the hospital staff had warned Helen that Mrs Miller might still be smoking sometimes on the sly, although it was smoking that had given her the emphysema which was slowly killing her.

26

Also, oxygen just taken in 'little whiffs' wasn't delivered in high enough concentrations to be effective against the low blood oxygen for which it was prescribed. No, Mrs Miller needed to use the equipment properly, and probably Nick ought to hear about those 'little whiffs', too.

She had spent half an hour with Mrs Miller now, and that would have to do for today. The elderly woman was getting very tired and breathless from talking. It had been a productive session, though slow-going, and Helen would have to sit at the nurses' station outside for several minutes to scribble notes on various aspects of the case before she forgot.

She had taken some notes while talking to the patient, too, but so often this tended to get in the way of the relaxed relationship she was trying to create in her role as health visitor and she had become skilled over the years at storing everything temporarily in her head until she could take the first opportunity to put it on paper.

She said goodbye to Mrs Miller, who responded kindly, 'Thanks for coming to see me, dearie,' as if she thought that Helen was someone who visited lonely hospital patients out of the goodness of her heart.

'I'll be seeing you again soon,' Helen responded.

Agatha's daughter, Barbara, would certainly need some strong support if she was to successfully look after the elderly woman in her own home. On the other hand, though, Mrs Miller had been at her brightest and most lucid when talking about her daughter and grandchildren, and that counted for a lot. Sketching out all this in her notes, Helen decided that she would give her backing to Barbara James's plan, provided the facilities in the James house were suitable.

Gloria Edmondson returned to the nurses' station just as Helen had written her final sentence and was closing her diary and case notebook.

'I was wrong earlier, Mrs Darnell,' the bright young

ward sister said. 'Dr Darnell *was* here. I hadn't seen him come in and I wasn't expecting him so, thanks to me, you missed him, I'm afraid.'

'Don't worry about it, Gloria,' Helen reassured her. 'I really didn't have anything special I needed to say to him.'

'No? Good, because I would have felt bad about it if you had.'

A minute later Helen had left the ward, wondering why she didn't have the same sense of insecurity about Gloria Edmondson as she did about Megan Stone. Gloria was also reasonably young, attractive, ambitious and apparently single.

So it's not simply that I'm jealous of any good-looking woman in his orbit, she decided. That was a relief! She had no desire to turn into a jealous harpy.

It was almost five o'clock when she got back to the office, and there was a phone message from Nick saying that he would be late home tonight—probably not until about seven-thirty. The knowledge that she had to wait another two and a half hours before she would see him didn't do anything to improve what had become a very unsettling day.

Helen looked at the backlog of work on her desk— record-keeping to catch up on, phone calls to make, school visits and case conferences to arrange—and made a sudden decision to shove it all aside for another day. With the twins gone now and Nick away from tomorrow until next Monday, she had the rest of the week to work late.

Instead, she made just one impulsive phone call—to her hairdresser—and was squeezed in for the last appointment of the day at six. She would have time to browse in the fashion boutique next door to the salon, and perhaps she would find some wonderful dress on sale. Her wardrobe badly needed restocking. . .

*   *   *

She *did* find something—a colourful print dress splashed with soft-toned flowers—and, though it didn't have the sophistication and tight, tailored elegance that Megan Stone favoured in her clothes, its open neck, figure-hugging waist and flowing skirt suited Helen's ripe, womanly figure and glossy halo of chestnut hair. She would wear it tonight and, with her new haircut and a delicious meal, the evening would have its dose of romance after all. Suddenly she really craved that.

Emerging from the hairdresser at a quarter to seven, with her full bob once again neatly shaped to her jawline, Helen didn't have a lot of time. Seven-thirty, Nick had said. She hurried home, put on the new dress and covered it carefully with an old gingham apron—already sadly stained as a result of its faithful service—then got to work.

A tossed salad, Danish fried potatoes, steamed asparagus and racks of lamb with hollandaise sauce. Ten past seven already. She had the potatoes parboiling and the racks of lamb beginning to sizzle in the oven. Now, recipe for the sauce? Ah, here!

Twenty past seven. 'Thicken, you cursed thing!' She was beating it with a hand whisk, and nothing seemed to be happening at all. Impatiently she turned the gas higher. It would have been nice to have time to redo her make-up and, heavens, she hadn't even begun to set the table prettily with a cloth and flowers and the best china as she had wanted to do.

The best china. . . It wasn't much and, in fact, a new dinner service was what they had sensibly agreed to give each other as an anniversary present as this was their china wedding anniversary. They had been planning to make a weekend of it and visit the Potteries in North Staffordshire but so far, with the Boston conference looming, there hadn't been time. Suddenly that seemed sad and unromantic—that they 'hadn't got around to' getting the gift to themselves that would seal this celebration.

And the hollandaise sauce had curdled. Ruthlessly she tipped it down the sink and began again. Patience this time! Only it was seven-thirty and the racks of lamb were done, the potatoes were falling apart and her only hope now was that Nick would be even later than he had predicted. Distractedly she brushed at an itch on her face and realised that she now had hollandaise sauce on her nose. She grabbed the front of her apron and wiped it away, not stopping to check in the hall mirror that it was all gone since she couldn't leave this wretched sauce.

That was Nick's car in the driveway now. Why was her heart hammering? She heard his key as she still whisked furiously at the sauce with a wrist that ached in protest. There was his rhythmic stride in the hall and the sound of his medical bag and leather briefcase, the latter heavy with papers, being dumped tiredly on the hall table.

'Home at last. Sorry!' He was in the kitchen doorway. . .and the hollandaise sauce had curdled again.

'You've had your hair cut.' She left the hated yellow glue bubbling on the stove and came towards him, badly needing the comfort of his familiar touch. Once in his arms she would tell him about that silly moment today when she hadn't recognised him, and they would both laugh.

'So have you,' he said. There! His arms were around her, strong and relaxed and loving. She rubbed her cheek cat-like against his.

'Hey! I don't want egg on my face, too!'

'What? Oh. . . Didn't I get it all off?' She pulled away and scrubbed with her apron again, until he gently took her hand away from her face, wet the corner of a linen tea-towel and did it for her. She closed her eyes and surrendered herself to the tenderness of the gesture.

'The kitchen's a bit of a bomb-site, darling.'

'I know. I've had a rotten day.'

'Rotten? What happened?'

And she couldn't think of a thing to say. Tell him about that stupid comment she had made to Marcella McPherson in front of everyone after lunch? No. Tell him about her suspicions in regard to Megan Stone's feelings for him? Heavens, no! Which only left her with the rather inane, 'I got home late, and now this special dinner isn't working out. I've overcooked the potatoes and curdled the hollandaise sauce twice!'

So perhaps it wasn't very surprising that he thought this no great tragedy. He drew away and, though she would have liked to nestle in his arms for minutes more, she straightened herself carefully as he said, 'Never mind. I've got to pack. Why don't you finish, and call me when it's done? No hurry. . .'

'Can't you pack tomorrow morning?' Can't you help me with the meal? Nick was handy in the kitchen when he had the time. Evidently he didn't now.

He made a face. 'Couple of patients I must see in the morning before I go. A new chap who I'm not very happy with. Wonder now whether I'm doing the right thing taking Megan, but it's an important conference for all sorts of reasons and she deserves this chance.'

'You've got Tony Glover covering for you, haven't you?'

'Yes, but his own case-load is pretty heavy. We need a third consultant. I'm hoping Megan will get her consultancy soon and we can bring in a couple of new people at the senior registrar level. She's working hard towards it but, of course, it's still a couple of years away. Meanwhile,' he sighed tiredly, 'I *must* go in tomorrow, and I'll go straight from the hospital to the station and get the train to Manchester Airport. So I'll pack until dinner's on the table, and then call me, hmm?'

'OK. . .'

He disappeared again, and she could hear him faintly in the bedroom, getting the suitcase down from the top of the built-in wardrobe and opening and shutting drawers, then going to the laundry to check that the shirts were dry in the airing cupboard. That's right, she'd have to iron them for him later on. . .

It was idiotic of her to feel so disappointed in the exchange that had just taken place. After all, what had she been hoping for? She thought about it as she threw out the hollandaise sauce for the second time and began again. Well, for a start he could have noticed her dress. And then perhaps he could have suggested that, since dinner was ruined and she looked so lovely, they could eat out.

'Be realistic, Helen,' she muttered. He obviously didn't have the time.

This time, by heroically reining her impatience and permitting no distractions, she made the hollandaise sauce successfully, then tossed the salad and heated a carton of fresh carrot soup, fried the rather soggy potatoes with onion, vinegar, mustard and sugar until they didn't look too bad, and flung a cloth, china and cutlery onto the dining-room table. It was funny to have Jon and Jane gone. The rosewood oval seemed too big for two. . .

'It's ready,' she called, and he came at once.

'Looks good.'

'The soup's not home-made, but it is that nice fresh kind from the fridge at the supermarket.'

'So you could have passed it off as home-made, and I'd never have known,' he teased drily.

And then the phone rang. Helen started to get up to answer it as Nick was looking so tired. If this was a medical matter, she'd deflect the call if she possibly could. Nick's SHO at the moment, Colin Hart, tended to seek advice far too often over trivial things, she considered. But, in spite of his fatigue, Nick got there first and it wasn't Colin at all—it was Jane. He didn't say her name, but she knew him so well that she could tell just from the sound of his voice—warmer, more relaxed and teasing.

He listened for a moment, exchanged some pleasantries, then said, 'Let's see now, what news is there?' He thought for a few seconds, then said with a teasing wisp of a grin, 'Pushcart's missing you, the old hypochondriac. . . No, I'm not joking; she's taken to self-diagnosis in the absence of your tender ministrations. I found her curled up asleep yesterday on top of one of my books, open at a page on pigeon breeder's disease. . .'

Helen glared at him and stifled a chuckle. Honestly! This was typical of his exchanges with Jane. Quite idiotic! The two of them had been in cahoots for years, particular on the issue of Pushcart—defending her against Jon's charge that she was getting revoltingly fat and Helen's anguish at the claw-marks on the legs of the dining table.

'No, she's not still catching them,' Nick was saying now. 'You know she's been too lazy to hunt for the past year or so. I think the last offering she presented to use was that poor field-mouse with the—' He broke off, catching Helen's impatient eye. She was longing to speak to her daughter. 'Hang on, I'm being signalled here.'

'I want to hear *her* news!' Helen interposed.

'Oh, right. Sorry.' And into the phone, 'What? No, I'm not asking the right questions, apparently. Let's see. . . What do we need to know? Um, are you washing your smalls? Taking your vitamins? Bringing apples for the teacher? Oops, now I'm being savagely threatened by a crazed woman.'

'Give me that phone!' She managed to seize it from him at last, pressed it to her ear and heard Jane's paroxysm of giggles at the other end of the line. 'Right, time for the serious conversation, madam. Nothing wrong, is there? Everything's all right?'

'No! Nothing's wrong!' came Jane's bubbly voice. 'I just wanted to wish you a happy anniversary, that's all.'

'You remembered? That's very sweet, love.' She asked about the preparations for university. It was scary having them both so far from home now but, according to Jane, both she and Jonathon had had no problems so far. Well, they'd only been on their own since Saturday afternoon!

'Not even homesick. . .much!' Jane added cheekily.

'Good,' Helen teased. 'Because I've already turned your room into a fully equipped Scandinavian sauna, so you can't come back!'

'Wonderful, Mum, a sauna every day will do you the world of good,' Jane returned calmly. 'But don't side-track me, I've got some news.'

'Oh, you have?'

'Yes. Russell and I are engaged! Isn't it wonderful? Just now, and I thought that was so romantic when I remembered it was your anniversary, I decided to ring straight away.'

It hit Helen like a blow from behind. Her stomach dropped like a stone and she couldn't even speak for a crucial half-minute. Motioning desperately to Nick who had gone to start wolfing down his soup through in the dining-room, she got him to take over again while she paced the hallway miserably, and his calm responses to their daughter were a background to Helen's wild thoughts.

Jane had only been going out with Russell Baldwin for two months. It wasn't that she was too young—after all, having married at seventeen herself, Helen could scarcely find fault on that score, although the illogical part of her screamed inwardly that Jane at eighteen was somehow *far* younger than Helen had been at seventeen! It was more that Russell was totally and utterly unsuitable and quite, quite wrong for her.

Jane was practical and sensible and was studying to be a vet. Russell was arty and wild and hadn't had a realistic idea in his life. Oh, he was quite sweet, not dangerous, dabbling in flute and sculpture and trying to get into a drama school in London. She could see the reason for the attraction of opposites on both sides, but. . . *engaged*? And what was Nick saying—so calmly and steadily?

'That's marvellous, darling. Congratulations! You'll have to bring him up when you come for a weekend, if he can make it.' There was a silence as Jane spoke at the other end, then, 'She wants you back, Helen,' and he passed the phone across again and went to the kitchen to bring out the napkins she had forgotten.

'I'm glad you're pleased, then,' Jane said. 'Actually, I thought Dad might be angry.'

'No, Dad doesn't seem to be angry,' Helen answered crisply. 'But I—' She stopped. Nick was glaring his disapproval at her as he returned to his soup.

'What, Mum?'

She sighed. Perhaps it was pointless to protest on the phone. 'Nothing, Jane. Look, we're just sitting down to dinner. I'll ring you tomorrow and we'll talk more then.'

'Don't,' Nick said, as soon as she'd put down the phone.

'Don't what?'

'Don't ring her tomorrow. Wait a bit.'

'Why?' she squeaked angrily. 'You can't be telling me you think this is *good* news!'

'Well, it's not *bad* news, is it, darling? She hasn't broken her leg. She's not in prison, she's not pregnant and she's not on drugs.' He ticked the items off on his fingers. 'She's just decided she wants to be engaged.'

'Yes, but—'

'Jane's a sensible girl, Helen.'

'Yes, I thought she was, but—'

'Leaving home can be tough. People react to it in different ways.'

'You think getting engaged is her reaction to leaving home?'

'I do, yes.'

'Rather extreme, surely?'

'Perhaps.' He shrugged and smiled.

'Don't you think we should try to talk her out of it? I mean, Russell is. . . You can't be suggesting that—'

'Let's not hash the whole thing over, Helen. Not now,' he interrupted. 'I've finished my soup and I've remembered something I need to jot down for the conference. Can you call me again when you're ready for the lamb, so we can eat together?'

He saw her look and added softly as he came round the table, massaging her shoulders briefly with his warm hands, 'Let's pretend this isn't our anniversary, hey? We'll have that when I get back from Boston. We'll go out to dinner and you can wear that delicious dress *without* a dirty apron on top!'

He kissed her neck, then left the room and she buried her face in her hands for a moment. So he had noticed the dress! And *she* had completely forgotten about this dreadful old apron, so she couldn't accuse him of being alone in his cavalier attitude to romance tonight.

She ate her soup without tasting it, aware of Nick in the study across the hall—scribbling memos to himself in his thick black diary. She couldn't blame him if he had to work tonight. The other conference delegates would scarcely excuse an ill-prepared speaker on the grounds that it had been his china wedding anniversary the night before he left.

What she couldn't understand, though, was his attitude to Jane's news. It would be a disaster if she and Russell got married, and Helen doubted that her daughter would last through a demanding course in veterinary medicine with Russell Baldwin permanently in tow. For a start, it seemed highly unlikely that his future plans included the possibility of supporting himself anywhere in the near future. Yet Nick seemed to approve!

She was frustrated that he hadn't wanted to talk about it, wanting badly to have him share her feelings about this. If they couldn't present a united front to Jane, what chance did they have of influencing her against the disastrous idea?

She sighed. It ought to get easier for married people to talk to each other as the years went by, but somehow it didn't. Oh, about the trivial things perhaps it did. She and Nick were a smoothly oiled machine when it came to arranging who would pick up the dry-cleaning or take Pushcart to the vet. Deeper things, though. . . Perhaps it was inevitable when you lived with someone for many years. She didn't want to seem like a nag or a shrew.

She finished her soup and called him back to the table, thinking again of Megan Stone and of that silly moment today when she hadn't recognised him in his new shirt and new haircut. Surely she ought to be able to talk to him about that! But, looking across at that strong, smooth face beneath its well-shaped helmet of dark hair, she couldn't find a way to say it. The outwardly trivial episode had suddenly become too important—a symbol of doubts about the health and success of their marriage which seemed to have grown out of nowhere, leaving her quite miserable and powerless to understand the strength of her own feelings.

He caught her brooding look and smiled helplessly, his even teeth very white and the little fans of wrinkles that formed at the corner of each eye only adding to the mature good looks of his face. A man was like a vintage wine, better and better with age. Was it the same for a woman?

'Sorry,' he said, his grey eyes liquid and deep. 'I'm thinking about the cases I want to highlight in my paper, wondering if I know enough about today's new admission to add him as an example. Can't tell you about it now. Too detailed, and my mind's a mess with it. Got to get it sorted out. Can you bear it if we don't talk?'

He reached across the table and touched her hand and she thought painfully, God, I love this man! Whatever else I'm doubting about our marriage at this moment, let me not doubt that!

They finished their meal at a quarter to nine, after decaffeinated coffee and a peach tart from the French bakery, and during dessert they *had* talked after all—about his flight tomorrow and the conference next week.

'It's important,' he said, 'because it's my chance to finalise this possibility of spending a year at Massachusetts State University Hospital.'

'Megan was talking about it today as if it's become more definite.'

'Yes, it's beginning to look that way, and she will probably be invited too. That's if we play our cards right at this conference—which, effectively, is being hosted by the chest department at MSUH. Megan did say she'd run into you.'

'Oh...yes,' Helen answered. Now was the time to tell him about that moment outside Mrs Gordon's room. Now... No, too late, he was speaking again.

'Anyway,' Nick concluded, 'there's no point in talking about what it would mean until it becomes more definite. Do I have your approval to push the idea, though? The money would be at least three times what I'm getting here, and the work would be fascinating.'

'Oh, obviously you should try as hard as you can to get it,' Helen said. 'There's be drawbacks, fairly important ones...'

'Of course. That's what we'd have to discuss.'

'Yes, I know I'd feel I was leaving part of myself—'

'But not now, I'm afraid...' He made a wry face. 'Um... Can you do my shirts?'

And so she spent the next hour and a quarter at the ironing-board and the sink, crisply pressing his shirts and cleaning up after the meal, while Nick could be heard in the study, sorting papers, scribbling notes and—at least twice—swearing volubly. At ten, tired, she began preparations for bed, taking off the light make-up she had worn during the day, brushing teeth and hair and hanging up the new dress.

Beneath her pillow was a plain, long-sleeved cotton nightdress in blue jersey knit and she reached for it, then paused. For her birthday in May Nick had given her a very different kind of nightdress, and she remembered Marcella McPherson with her pink bag from the lingerie boutique. She had no idea when Nick would be coming to bed, but. . .

Slowly she went to the drawer and took out his gift. It was cream silk and cotton lace and, taking off her underclothing, she stood before the mirror and held it against her body, feeling the whisper of the silk on her skin falling to her calves. It felt so wonderful, but she didn't wear it all that often as it had to be hand-washed and, really, it seemed too expensive and lovely just to wear to *bed*, and. . .and. . .

Her own prosaic attitude suddenly shamed her and she slipped the silken sheath over her body. Its thin lace straps left her shoulders bare and the gathering beneath the soft triangular cups emphasised the fullness of her breasts, which Nick had always gloried in. The lace left little to the imagination, and the golden light from the bedside lamp cast its shadow across the front of her body, making the valley between the two ripe shapes look deep and inviting and painting a sheen on the fabric across the gentle curve of her stomach.

She looked at her figure and her face in the mirror and thought to herself, I'm not so bad for thirty-seven. . . in this light. Her hair was still rich and glossy, her body had carried and borne twins but it didn't really show. She was a little heavier around the hips than she had been twenty years ago and, of course, there were wrinkles, but they came more from laughter than frowning. No, not so bad for thirty-seven. . .

She climbed into bed and turned out the light, hoping that Nick would come soon and intending to wait for him—but inexorably sleep began to creep over her. Why was it that when she wanted to stay awake she got help-lessly drowsy at once, and when she particularly needed to get a good night she often lay awake for. . .

Her sleepy mind couldn't even finish the thought.

She did not know what time it was when she stirred to find Nick sliding in beside her, but when she drowsily realised that he was naked she gave a little smile and nestled against him so that they fitted each other's shapes like spoons in a cutlery drawer.

'Mmm. . .this,' he said throatily, running a warm hand along the curve of her hip so that the silk slipped against her skin. He rolled back a little and pulled her with him so that she was half lying on him now and his arms were around her, holding her just where the heavy curves beneath her breasts spilled against him.

She turned into his arms, exulting in the fact that they were about to make love and needing it with an intensity that had her trembling. This part of their marriage had always been good. In the beginning it had been white-hot, and even as the years went by it had retained its magic—been like an oasis for them both. Inevitably, though. . .

Often they were both so tired, and as the twins grew older there came the awareness that they were not alone in the house and could not surrender themselves to the wildfire passion that had once come at any hour of the night or day. They both knew, without saying anything about it, that the frequency and spontaneity of their love-making had lessened over the years.

In this moment none of that seemed to matter. He was holding her, burying his face in her neck, kissing her shoulders and her lips hotly, then travelling downwards to pillow his head between her breasts. She held him even more closely, tracing pathways in his fragrant hair with her fingertips and opening her legs to wrap them around his strong thighs.

'Will you come to Boston as my mistress, you volumptuous creature?' he whispered, heated and teasing at the same time.

'Mistress? . . . *Volumptuous*?'

'Sumptuous, voluptuous. It ought to be a word, even if it isn't. And in this bit of nothing you're far too sexy to be anyone's wife. No one at the conference would believe me, so I'd have no alternative but to introduce you. . .as my mistress.'

'Oh, Nick, I love you so much,' she whispered.

He answered her with his lips, lapping hungrily at her own mouth and drawing a wild response from her, and then she was lost in a maelstrom of touch and taste and sensation, clinging to him desperately and abandoning herself to sheer physical need until their shared climax came and they lay still, both breathless and replete.

Almost immediately he was asleep, his head on her shoulder and his hand cupping her breast as it always did. The straps of her nightdress had slipped down so that there was no barrier to his touch, and for several minutes she just lay there dreamily and watched that warm, familiar hand holding her fullness. There was a smile on his face—she knew it, although she could not see it—and she did not mind the fact that he slept. It wasn't selfish abandonment—just a sign that, as she did, he felt utterly relaxed and safe in her arms.

Then suddenly he had jerked awake, as if roused by a startling image in a dream, and she could feel the difference in him—the tension in his muscles, the mental preoccupation. 'Damn!' he muttered.

'What?' Her voice was creaky.

'I've remembered something else. . .' And already he had rolled out of bed and was getting back into his clothes, dragging them on impatiently and frowning into the darkness. 'I meant to spend the afternoon on all this, but with this new patient. . .' And he had gone without any further explanation.

The bed was cold and lonely now, and Helen had

lost her dreaminess. She felt uncomfortable and a little ridiculous with the silk nightdress bunched at her waist and pulled down below her breasts. Her nipples were tight with cold now, not passion, and she got out of bed and took off the flowing sheath of silk to dive into the blue cotton knit she had earlier disdained. She wanted Nick still to be here and, though she accepted that he had to go and complete the task he had remembered, she rebelled in a childish way and felt angry with the whole universe.

'I needed him here tonight. I needed us to fall asleep together. . .'

And, of course, now she found that she couldn't go to sleep at all. Hadn't too much of their marriage been like this? There had always been something to get in the way of the time they should have had just to themselves.

It was a legacy of marrying young, of course. Nick's mother and father, who were now dead, had not been well off and her own parents, while not completely opposed to the early marriage, had believed that if she and Nick were so determined not to wait then they had to be prepared to take the financial consequences.

And those consequences had been heavy. With Nick still a medical student and she just out of school and completely untrained, their income had been minimal for the first few years. She had worked in a florist's until the twins arrived and had begun her nursing training when they'd started school at five years of age, after exhausting herself with poorly paid part-time work at odd hours during their toddler years.

Looking back on the twenty years of her marriage, it seemed tonight as if the time had passed in a constant whirl of juggling. Juggling time, juggling money, juggling debt and work and child-care. They had burdened themselves with the mortgage on this house as soon as they could scrape together a deposit and, though in the long run it was sensible and had saved them money, for several years it had only added to the pressure. The twenty-year mortgage was nearly paid off now, and Helen thought to herself, Well, that's an achievement out of all that penny-pinching. A house in our names, free and clear.

Only she didn't actually like the house.

No, nonsense! Of course she did! It was practical and adequate in size, and the flat aprons of lawn at front and back, bordered with narrow, tidy beds for shrubs and flowers, were easy to maintain. . .

She *didn't* like the house! At least be honest about it, since today she seemed to be questioning everything. It was *too* practical! It was boring, and really rather ugly since, when it came to furniture and decorating, they were always promising themselves that 'one day', when they were out of debt and had more time, they'd do it all properly.

Helen rolled over in bed, restless and miles from sleep, tears pinching in her eyes. 'What is *wrong* with me?' she whispered aloud to the dark room. 'What is wrong with my life? If I told Nick about all this, would he think I was being idiotic?'

He certainly hadn't seemed too sympathetic over the issue of Jane's engagement, she remembered, and added that to her baggage of things to worry about. She could hear him in the study, opening and shutting his briefcase. Not very far away. Just a room away. Yet it suddenly felt like miles, and tomorrow night it *would* be miles— thousands of them. 'Oh, God, what's happening to us?'

When he finally came to bed she was still awake but she pretended not to be and he didn't try to touch her, just lay well to the far side and buried his head in the soft feather pillows with a deep sigh. Five minutes later she heard the rhythmic breathing that told her he was asleep.

CHAPTER THREE

HELEN overslept. She awoke at seven-thirty to find Nick shaking her shoulder gently as he bent towards her. Opening her eyes, she saw that he was fully dressed in the dark business suit he had chosen for the flight.

'I have to go.'

'Oh, already?' She struggled to sit up.

''Fraid so. There's coffee still in the pot. I'll miss you, darling.'

'Ring me when you get to the hotel.'

'Of course. See you next week.' He bent closer and kissed her swiftly on the mouth, then left the room while she was still fighting the need to cling to him and feverishly demand his words of love.

She remembered that he hadn't actually said he loved her last night, in response to her own tremulous phrase, only seeming to show it with his body and with that typically frivolous comment about being his mistress. Then, that had been enough. Now, she couldn't help dwelling on it. A man could lie with his body, driven by physical need. Nick hadn't actually told her he loved her for a while. Perhaps he assumed that she knew it deep in her bones.

Or perhaps he took both his love and hers so much for granted that he didn't really feel it any more. Perhaps he hadn't realised this yet but if Megan Stone had anything to do with it he would, and he was about to spend the next six and a half days with Megan, staying in the same hotel an ocean away from his wife and his home. . .

Irritated with herself for the gloomy view she was taking of things, Helen got abruptly out of bed, showered, dressed and ate breakfast alone in the kitchen, noting that Nick had washed up his own things. Normally she would have taken this as a sign of his consideration and loved him for it. Today it seemed like a distancing action, as if the two of them were like the students sharing Jon and Jane's digs—independent, self-sufficient, unconnected.

Separate dishes, separate shelves in the fridge. . . That was all right for students, but for husbands and wives? Some couples *did* live that way. To stubborn, too lazy or too embarrassed to get divorced, as Megan had suggested yesterday—living beneath the same roof but eating separate meals, doing separate loads of laundry, leading separate lives.

'Give me a clean divorce any day!' Helen told her coffee.

And suddenly she found that she was thinking of it. What would happen? How would it work? Well, he could buy her out of the house, for a start. No arguments there. Except that she doubted that someone like, say, Megan Stone, would want to live here. A streamlined flat would be more her style. And perhaps that would suit Nick, too. He sometimes grouched about mowing the lawn. Over the years, the uninspiring garden had always been mainly for the children.

The children. They were essentially grown up now. No contests over custody. Jon and Jane could pay visits to each parent whenever they chose. Pushcart? She was getting very old, the plump tabby puss, and she'd probably prefer to stay with the house. In any case, she'd only last a couple more years.

Good heavens, in practical terms, getting a divorce would be easy! There was nothing holding them together at all. It could be all quite neat and civilised and, since she'd always worked, she wouldn't even have the difficult transition that Stella Harris had had into financial independence.

Helen was weak-kneed when she rose from the kitchen

table to do her own sparse collection of dishes. A divorce would be so easy for Nick and herself that it was quite frightening and horrible, and the thought that there might be chinks in the armour of his love that would allow Megan to have her wistful way with him had assumed the proportions of a nightmare in her mind now.

If Nick had still been here. . . If there had been something to distract her—Jonathon and Jane chattering about sports, or asking what was for dinner. But she was alone, the twins were gone—well embarked on the challenging journey towards full adulthood—and she wouldn't see Nick for almost a week. Shaken, miserable and still preoccupied, Helen got ready for work and left the house.

Calling in at the office first, she then had a full morning of home visits planned, including one to Barbara James's house to assess the possibility of Agatha Miller being looked after in her daughter's home. She intended to make this call first and then do the rounds of the underfives on her list but Dr Snaith, the boyish-faced but very competent GP who most often added patients to her caseload, beckoned her into his surgery as soon as she arrived.

'Got someone new for you, Helen,' he told her. 'I've just been on the phone to your better half about it.'

'To Nick? He did mention he had a new patient. He's still at the hospital, then? He'll be cutting it fine for getting his train.'

'That's right, he's off across the Atlantic today, isn't he? Why don't you head straight up, then, and you'll probably catch him. He can tell you all about it. Basically, it's a TB case. . .'

'TB? Where do I come in, then?' Helen asked.

'Poor compliance, and Nick wants to put him under directly observed therapy once he's discharged. I gather there's an attitude problem and he feels you're the one this chap's most likely to accept. I saw the man yesterday and referred him straight up to Nick at the hospital. He was admitted, and—'

'I *will* go straight away, then,' Helen interrupted. Steve Snaith was always ready for a natter, and the possibility of seeing Nick again before he left for the airport was making her impatient to get to the hospital. It would be too awful if she just missed him.

'Right you are, then,' Dr Snaith nodded cheerfully, as Helen quickly adjusted the morning's schedule in her mind. She'd ring Barbara James and see if it was all right to come just after lunch, instead. . . 'I'll let Nick fill in the details.'

Helen picked up her diary, notebook and bag and hurried straight out to the car, thinking far more about Nick than about this new patient. She couldn't remember exactly the time of the train he had been planning to catch, but she thought it was very soon. Perhaps he had decided to risk a later one and cut it a little finer at Manchester airport.

At the hospital she went straight up to the men's side of the chest ward and again was greeted by a ward sister whom she had met before, Karen Graham, in the same way that Gloria Edmondson had greeted her yesterday. 'Are you looking for Dr Darnell?'

This time the answer was 'Yes,' but again the ward sister's next words were disappointing.

'I'm not sure. He *was* here, and I'm sure he hasn't really *gone*, if you know what I mean.'

'Could he be with the patient I'm supposed to see?'

'Now, who's that?'

'New. Tuberculosis.'

'Oh, Paul Chambers!' She laughed and looked a little flustered. 'Yes, he's in Room Nine.'

'That's one of the new privates, isn't it?'

'Yes. Second on the left. And put on a surgical mask. There's a box of them just outside his door.'

Helen turned the corner in the corridor and found the room, her first feeling on entering it being one of disappointment as Nick wasn't there and the patient was alone. Her next feeling, though, as she put on the confining mask. . .

Paul Chambers was utterly unlike the sketchy preconception she had formed of a TB patient who was complying poorly with taking the barrage of antibiotics that would get rid of the disease. Since the advent of drugs that attacked Mycobacterium tuberculosis earlier this century, TB sufferers in the United Kingdom had tended to be poor and elderly, or immigrants from poverty-stricken nations. However, since the alarming resurgence of the disease that had begun in the 1980s, some HIV-positive drug-users and prison inmates had been added to this group.

This man was none of these things, at least at first glance. Tall and powerfully built, in spite of the weight loss so often associated with TB, he had a ruthlessly intelligent face and looked to be in his early forties. His good looks were the rugged kind that went with a large dose of arrogance and rebelliousness. There was a potent and aware sexuality to him as well, and he turned it full onto Helen as soon as he saw her.

'Well, now, who's this?' A drawl and a wicked smile as he flicked an appreciative gaze over her ripe figure. 'A hospital volunteer, come to bring me magazines? I'm not sure that I'm allowed to have them. I'm supposed to be infectious, you know. I contaminate at a touch.'

'Yes, I *do* know, as I'm a nurse—not a volunteer,' Helen answered crisply, through the barrier of her mask. 'But TB isn't spread through hand-to-hand contact, so I imagine magazines would be no problem.'

'A woman of sense at last! Now, I ask you!' He spread his huge hands, and his blue eyes bored into hers. 'Do I look as though I have TB?'

'No, you don't,' she began.

He came in quickly, 'And yet I *do* have it. Call it a war wound.'

'A war wound?' Unwillingly she was intrigued by the

phrase, with its aura of suffering in a noble cause. Quite an intriguing man. . .

'Yes. Now, who are you, exactly?' The change of subject teased her, as it was meant to. 'You said a nurse, but you're not in uniform like these other goodly souls.'

'No, I don't wear a uniform. I'm a health visitor,' she explained lightly.

'Which means?'

'I spend most of my time in the community, involved in disease prevention and health education, and care and support in times of illness and stress—particularly with under-fives.'

'Now, where do I fit into that lot, I wonder?' Again, his intelligent blue eyes bored into hers, glinting with wicked humour. 'I'm not under five, and you can't prevent my disease because I already have it. Health education? That doesn't sound like me either. Which leaves care and support.' His voice dropped very low. 'Have you really come to *care* about me, Helen?'

'How did you know my name was—? Oh, you were told I was coming.' So much for thinking she was a volunteer!

'I was,' he acknowledged, 'by your fine upstanding husband, who *didn't* tell me, by the way, what a charming and attractive wife he had.'

Helen gasped as Paul Chambers suddenly prowled down upon her, took her hand in his powerful grip and brought it to his lips, looking over it through his fringe of sooty lashes to meet her startled gaze. She was frozen into immobility for several seconds, and he took advantage of this to murmur, 'My neighbour mentioned you, too, when she happened to come past this morning. Stella's a colleague of yours, I understand.'

'Helen!' Nick was in the doorway. She hadn't heard his approach at all! Like lightning, she whisked her hand free of Paul Chambers's grip, and felt the deliberate caress of his thumb as she did so.

'Nick, I—I was hoping to see you.' She sounded and felt flustered. Why hadn't she twisted her hand out of that wicked contact at once? Of course Nick would understand that she hadn't wanted it, but. . .

Except that he *didn't* seem to understand. His grey eyes, usually so warm and tender, were like cold steel and his mouth was set hard. 'I need to speak to you.'

'Of course.'

She started out of the room at once, but had time to hear Paul Chambers drawl behind her, 'Didn't mean to cause trouble.'

'What on earth did you do that for?' Nick rasped at her as soon as they had moved out of the patient's earshot down to the end of the corridor.

'*I* didn't do it! *He* did! I did nothing.'

'You let him.'

'I didn't have a chance to. . .to. . .' She was angry now herself, and shaking, unable to find the right words.

A scene with Nick! Such a rarity, really, in their interactions together. And it had to come now! She knew that she looked guilty. She *felt* guilty! The man had mentioned Stella just then, with a distinctly knowing air, and she realised with horror that this must be the neighbour Stella was suggesting she ogle. . .or have an affair with. And, though it was the last thing she wanted, she couldn't deny that she had been aware of the man's potent sexuality. How could she have been otherwise when, clearly, it was something he turned on deliberately, using it as a weapon or as camouflage—like some chemical spray?

That she was aware of it didn't mean that she was susceptible to it, and already she had no illusions about the kind of man Paul Chambers was. Why, he was even using his disease to create a cloak of glamour and importance. 'War wound,' indeed! He was good at it, though, because unwillingly she was still curious as to what he had meant by the term.

'I didn't want it!' she protested hotly once again.

'Really, Nick, he just kissed my hand. We're not having an affair!'

His eyes narrowed. 'An *affair*?' An impatient sigh hissed between his teeth. 'Helen, there's a very strong possibility that this man has a multi-drug-resistant strain of TB imported from the ghettos of New York. I'm taking absolutely no chances with it from now on, and I suggest you don't either. We've started a contact tracing, and I've just ordered complete respiratory isolation. Negative air-flow through his room, a complete air-exchange six times every hour—an extra fan will be fitted today—and particulate respirators to be worn by staff in his room at all times. Now, I've got to go.'

He made to turn away, but she grabbed his arm. 'Nick. . .' She didn't know what she wanted to say. Please don't be angry. What I said about an affair was stupid. Don't we have time to talk for a minute before you go? Kiss me! With all these demands and entreaties whirling in her brain, nothing came out.

'I have to go.'

'Your train, I know, but—'

'No, Megan's going to drive me. She's already gone to get the car. She'll be waiting below with the engine running, so you see. . .'

'Megan?'

'I hadn't realised she was planning to drive. I thought we'd both be on the train. I'll ring you. Bye. . .'

Nick's kiss was a brief feathering on her cheek and then he was gone and she couldn't run after him, calling his name like in some bad TV adaptation of *Wuthering Heights*. He was going away for a week. Less than a week. Six days. That was no tragedy.

And yet the thought that she wouldn't see him for nearly a whole *week* had made such a lump in her throat that she could barely swallow. It wasn't not seeing him, it was parting in anger. They'd been away from each other before, and for longer periods than a week. When his mother had died, for example, and once when she'd visited her own parents, now in Devon, for a two-week holiday with the children. But they'd never before parted in anger.

Megan was driving him to the airport. That was another thing she couldn't help hating and dwelling on. Well, it would have been silly for Megan to drive and Nick to take the train when they were leaving from the same place and catching the same flight. But she couldn't get rid of the image of the two of them, cocooned alone in Megan's sleek scarlet car, with travel and a conference to look forward to, and only the image of a shrewishly indignant wife left behind.

On his way down in the lift Nick remained more than a little irritable—with Helen, with himself and with the world in general. He understood why she was emotional but, because he didn't have time to help her through it, he illogically wished that she could have postponed her feelings.

It worried him more than a little, this feeling that her reaction to the twins' departure made her something like a powder keg. Or a string of fireworks, perhaps. She might go off at any time, and in quite an unpredictable direction. His dry humour asserted itself for a moment. Perhaps she'd run away to join a colony of travellers, or start singing to her herbs?

He was missing the twins himself, and was aware that it was influencing his moods as well. For a start, he shouldn't have snapped at Helen like that just now! And this conference should be happening a month from now, so that he could insist that she came too! And if this business of Paul Chambers blew up into something serious. . .

Emerging from the front entrance, Nick saw Megan's car as she waved and tooted, and a moment later he had slid into the passenger seat beside her. Colourfully and attractively dressed, she wore a smile of suppressed excitement on her face. Her mood of anticipation was infectious and for the first time he really registered, We're going to Boston today. It'll be good to get away from the hospital. I need a break from the stress and the routine.

'I've been looking forward to this for months!' she said as she drove off, and he chuckled.

'Your enthusiasm is good for me, Megan.'

'Is it?' She took it as a compliment, which he supposed it was, and her smile—which could sometimes be oddly hesitant—brightened still further.

'America will love you,' he told her kindly, then remembered two particular Americans—colleagues— who wouldn't be at the conference. Did he have their phone numbers? He checked the small address book in his breast pocket. So much to keep track of. He really *must* remember to phone them. . . Checking his mental list for the tenth time, he was unaware of the glowing smile which still shone on Megan's lovely face.

Going up to Karen Graham at the nurses' station, immediately after her scene with Nick, Helen couldn't help sounding a little sharp when she asked, 'Why didn't you tell me that Paul Chambers is in complete respiratory isolation?'

'Oh. . . Dr Darnell only just ordered it. Did you see him?'

'Only for a minute. He didn't have time to tell me much.' We just shouted at each other. 'You'll have to fill me in now.'

'He and Dr Glover have been talking about it all morning,' the fair, plumply pretty ward sister said. 'They've taken cultures in order to isolate the strain of the bacterium, but that takes two to four weeks at least to yield a result, apparently, so they're trying some ''detective work'', they said. Dr Darnell didn't tell me what he meant by that.'

'What makes them suspect an MDR strain in the first place?'

'He's a journalist and writer. You know, one of those in-depth kind. He's been doing a book on homelessness and drug abuse in New York, and actually living with some of the people he's researching. He's a fascinating man.' Helen now recognised the faint blush as Karen Graham's consciousness of Paul Chambers's deliberate sexuality. 'Anyway, he contracted TB some months ago but—I don't know—for some reason he wasn't able to complete his drug therapy in America. He thought he'd beaten it but now he's back here, writing up the book in peace and quiet, and he noticed that the symptoms had returned.'

'And New York is one of the places where these multi-drug-resistant strains have been found,' Helen mused.

Tuberculosis was Nick's special field. His fellow chest physicians had been sceptical fifteen years ago when he had begun to develop this research interest.

'Not exactly a growth industry, old man. It'll be like smallpox by the end of the century—eradicated world-wide,' one colleague had said.

But Nick's answer, often-repeated, now seemed very prophetic. 'I think you're wrong,' he had said. 'I see an elderly patient forgetting to take her drugs properly, or losing one batch and thinking the other three will surely do the trick just as well. Or I see a doctor tinkering with the regime, deciding to lower the dose or leave out two of the first-line antibiotics and let another two do the job on their own. In some countries it might happen purely because they're trying to spread scarce and expensive drugs too thinly.

'And what I see are human Petri dishes, in which it's only a matter of time before super-bacteria develop that are resistant to all those first-line agents, and then what's going to happen? Believe me, the misuse of antibiotics in modern medical practice is going to cause major problems down the line, and TB is *not* going to be eradicated in the foreseeable future!'

And then, several years ago, what Nick and others had predicted started to happen—amongst the poor populations of countries such as China, but also in richer nations such as Britain and the United States. Intravenous drug use, urban poverty and AIDS were all contributing factors.

Although Nick didn't come across many patients in his own practice with these additional problems, his meticulous documentation of the kinds of TB cases he did see, his participation in clinical trials for the British Medical Research Council and his extensive research into the changing epidemiology of the disease had taken him to conferences all over the country.

It was his research interest in TB that the Department of Thoracic Medicine at Massachusetts State University Hospital was interested in, and Helen knew that he was far more excited about the possibility of working in Boston for a year, and possibly longer, than he had expressed aloud.

Now it seemed that in Paul Chambers Nick might have on his hands a case of the MDR TB he had foreseen. It was understandable, then, that he was extremely concerned about the possibility of the disease spreading to any of the health workers involved in treating the new patient. And it wasn't just a theoretical risk. There were many documented cases of this happening in the United States.

'Do you know exactly how Nick envisages my involvement with this patient?' Helen asked Karen Graham.

'No, I don't, I'm afraid.' She made a face. 'The timing has been bad, hasn't it? He was only admitted yesterday afternoon, after he went to his GP with the symptoms, and of course Dr Darnell has been so busy preparing for this conference. I know we've got him on a barrage of antibiotics and he's under directly observed therapy.

'I think at this stage Dr Darnell just wants you to talk to him and gain his approval and confidence, find out what makes him tick and if it'll be safe to discharge him once he's no longer infectious—or if he's likely to skip town and put others in danger by stopping his treatment. If he remains under directly observed therapy once he is discharged, I should think Dr Darnell will want you to be the observer.'

'It's in the active phase, obviously?'

'Oh, my goodness, yes. Vile fits of coughing. He's such a big man, in spite of the weight loss, and he sounds like a truck motor that won't start.'

'Nasty!' Helen exclaimed. Karen Graham's simile was a vivid one.

'Yes,' the latter nodded, grimacing. 'He must be embarrassed about it, too, because he always goes into his bathroom if he feels it coming on. We've got strict protocols for disposing of anything he brings up and, as you know, he's in complete respiratory isolation now.'

'I'll spend a bit more time with him now, then, and see if I can find out any more from Nick tonight when he rings me from Boston.' She was counting the hours already until she could start expecting his call. Probably not until eight or nine tonight.

'Go ahead, then,' Karen nodded. 'One thing, though. . .'

'Mmm?'

'From what I've seen so far, the less you treat him like a patient the more success you'll have with him.'

'Hmm, that sounds a bit dangerous.'

'I think he's a dangerous man, Mrs Darnell.' The pink came and went in the ward sister's cheeks. 'That's part of the problem!'

So Helen braved Paul Chambers's personality again.

He was looking flushed and bright-eyed now, and breathing more heavily as he prowled his private room restlessly. 'Have you been coughing?' she asked him at once, then bit her lip. This was *not* what Karen Graham had just advised.

'Bit.' Very off-hand.

He sat down in the chair beneath the small high window, where a second, more powerful exhaust fan was to be fitted that afternoon, and looked at her defiantly, so she changed her approach to say lightly and with almost a hint of flirtation, 'So, tell me about this war wound of yours!'

And within a few minutes she knew indisputably that Karen Graham's comment had been very perceptive. He *was* a dangerous man. Fancying himself very much as a hero and a soldier of fortune, the profession of modern investigative journalist suited him down to the ground. He had spent extensive periods of time in all sorts of trouble-spots all over the world and his tales of the six months he had lived in the worst parts of New York, gathering material for the book he was now writing, were both harrowing and fascinating.

As she listened to him Helen had to fight, sometimes, to remember why she was here. This wasn't raconteurship to be enjoyed after dinner over a glass of port. By his own admission this man had failed to complete the drug regimen necessary to cure a contagious and potentially fatal disease, and Helen could now see that he really believed himself to be invincible. In fact, he almost seemed to enjoy the fact that he was flirting with death and, on impulse, she suddenly asked, 'So, is this going to be the sequel to your book about the underbelly of New York? The story of your own fight against a deadly strain of TB?'

Paul Chambers threw back his head and laughed. 'It'd work, wouldn't it? If the first book sells—and it will. There's all sorts of material I'm having to put aside because it doesn't quite belong in *The Beggars of Broadway*. What better way to unify all that left-over stuff than within the dramatic structure of my own odyssey—getting cured of TB. It'll be a best-seller.'

'Provided you don't get cured too quickly,' she put in even more crisply. 'Not much drama in a successful nine months of broad-spectrum antibiotic treatment.'

His eyes had narrowed now, and he drawled in a rough tone, 'Well, I wouldn't put it in quite those terms, but, yes. My treatment has had its ups and downs. This disease take some beating. But modern medicine triumphs in the end. That'll be the thrust of it. This is the disease that felled a dozen of my literary heroes in the past. My victory over it will be the highest tribute I can pay those heroes, surely! What a great theme!'

'Always assuming you live long enough to write the book.'

She couldn't help it; she had angered him, and she didn't care. The way this man insisted on romanticising himself, placing himself at the centre of a drama and deliberately intensifying the experience, was dangerous and wrong. Not just dangerous to himself but to others as well, including the staff on this ward who were putting themselves at risk—albeit, taking all the precautions they could—in order to treat him.

He was glaring at her now, and in the back of her mind was the knowledge that she hadn't exactly followed the doctor's orders. Nick had wanted her to gain this man's approval and confidence, and instead it almost looked as if he was about to order her out of the room.

'Of course I'll damn well live long enough to write the book,' he growled, half rising in his chair and his blue eyes spitting sparks. He looked very big and powerful in that moment, in spite of his disease, his jaw as angular as a brick, his gaze boring right into her and his bony shoulders broad. With such physical and mental strength, and the bravery he had undoubtedly needed to call upon in the past, no wonder he had the illusion that he was invincible!

Helen met his stare full on, her own green eyes as steady as his. 'Of course you will,' she agreed in a clear, strong voice. 'You're far too intelligent to do anything as stupid as messing around with your treatment regimen *again*!'

For a moment he didn't answer. He had already subsided in his chair and now those powerful shoulders were hunched as he was seized by a fit of coughing. Suddenly the aura of invincibility was gone, and Helen saw stark fear in his face for the first time.

'Get out,' he bawled, as he seized a sputum cup from on top of the small chest of drawers beside his bed. 'Just go, will you, Nurse?'

Helen was shaken by the encounter, and it took several innocuous visits to some of the under-fives and their mothers on her list before she had fully recovered. Stella's notion that she have an affair with this man was utterly ludicrous. Aside from any other considerations— such as the fact that Helen herself was in love with her husband, and Paul Chambers was a patient with a life-threatening and contagious disease—it would be an act of pure self-injury on her part.

The man was completely self-obsessed, and any woman who became involved with him would soon become a mere hand-maiden to his ego and his image. She thought of the way Karen Graham had blushed so prettily when she talked about the new patient. She had acknowledged that he was 'dangerous' but Helen had a sudden horrible foreboding that Karen was far from immune to the true nature of the danger, even though she dimly perceived it.

'She's attracted to him, although she doesn't quite know it yet,' Helen said aloud as she parked her Crown car outside Barbara James's modest suburban home after a quick sandwich lunch in the car. 'I hope he doesn't

see it because he'll use the fact to his own ends if he
needs to!'

Wondering whether she could or should try to com-
municate all these insights to Nick, Helen walked up the
path to the Jameses' house, then took a deep breath and
dismissed Paul Chambers from her mind as she thought
about her next case.

It was a successful visit. Barbara's house was tidy and
efficiently organised, but not so much as to lead to the
suspicion that it was all just for show today because she
had known Helen was coming. The dining-room that
opened between the family-sized kitchen and comfortable living-room had been set up as a bedroom for Agatha
Miller, with the door to the living-room now blocked off
by a piano. 'Otherwise the kids'll just use the room as
a passageway,' Barbara explained, 'and Mum needs her
privacy.'

There was a lavatory on the ground floor, so the only
reason for Mrs Miller to make the tiring journey upstairs
was to have a shower or bath.

'The kids are looking forward to it already,' Barbara
enthused. 'Even though I've explained to them that Gran
can't do much and she's going to need a lot of rest
and quiet.'

Helen made her suggestion that the two children be
brought in to the hospital one afternoon to be made
familiar with the oxygen equipment which Mrs Miller
would be bringing home with her, and also alerted
Barbara to the potential problem of the 'little whiffs'.

'Oh, I know,' Barbara said, throwing up her hands.
'That's one of the reasons I want to have her. She's
always been like that—*very* creative about pill-taking
and so forth; thinks up her own variations on the treat-
ments. No, don't worry, I'll make sure she uses that
venturi mask!'

'And how is your husband feeling about all this?'

'Oh, supports it in theory, though he's like most men—

a bit wary of his mother-in-law. He knows he'd want to do the same for his mum if she needed it. Fortunately she doesn't at this stage. Fit as a fiddle. No, my biggest worry,' Barbara went on, 'is. . .that!'

She gestured out of the kitchen window to a very pleasant little half-screened back porch, which would trap the warmth deliciously on sunny days. Even with today's clouds and wind it looked inviting, with its two wicker armchairs and jungle of potted plants.

Helen was confused. 'Your mother doesn't like the porch?'

'Oh, she loves it! And I *know* she's going to sneak out there and smoke in that chair whenever I'm not looking, I just know it.'

'Hmm. . .' Helen frowned. 'There's not a lot we can do about that, is there?'

'No. She's about as obedient to me as I was to her when I was two! It comes full circle, doesn't it?' Barbara smiled ruefully.

Helen left soon afterwards, noting that Barbara seemed pleasant and sensible and well aware of the potential pitfalls in what she was trying to do. The idea of forming a chronic emphysema support group began to seem more and more compelling, however. Nick would certainly thank her if it resulted in any emphysema sufferers giving up smoking.

Nick. . . She looked at her watch and found that it was already after two. Only six hours, perhaps, until she would hear his voice. Soft this time, she hoped, not with the harshness of the anger he had shown her this morning.

She continued to count the hours for the rest of the day and arrived home at her silent house at half past six, having stayed late at the office to catch up on things, since there'd been no reason to hurry home. The cat to feed, eggs for tea, and Nick couldn't possibly ring yet. His plane would still be in the air, beginning its descent to Boston airport.

Ring Jon and Jane, then? It was very tempting. Find out if Jonathon had done as promised and bought himself some half-decent clothes. Try to reason with Jane about this idiotic engagement to Russell Baldwin. Nick had told her not to. Nick, in fact, had been horribly obtuse and lacking in sympathy about the whole thing! Stubbornly she set her jaw and made the call, her mind already busy with the perfectly worded phrases she would use to present her compelling argument.

Only, of course, when Jane came on the phone, breathless and announcing in her first sentence that she was on the point of going out, none of the perfectly worded phrases would come and Helen could only say in a tone high with pleading, '*Don't* go through with this engagement idea, Jane. He's all wrong for you and I know it'll end badly. Marriage is a serious business and— It's not that we don't like him. It's just that you're young and—'

Mistake.

'I'm eighteen months older than you were when you got engaged to Dad, Mum.'

It went downhill from there, and she could only be thankful that Nick hadn't heard the phone call. Hadn't he told her that any attempt to reason with Jane would only make things worse? By the time she had finished pacing the kitchen, waiting for the kettle to boil and fuming impotently over her call to Jane, Helen was counting the minutes until eight o'clock.

CHAPTER FOUR

'SORRY I couldn't ring earlier. . .' When Nick's voice came at last, it was after half past nine. 'The flight was a bit late and, what with Customs and Baggage Claim and whatnot, we've only just got in.'

'You sound tired.'

'Of course! But we'll unpack and then get something to eat. It's nearly a quarter to five here. We're going to try to hold off on sleep until something resembling local bedtime, and hopefully get a good night before the first session at nine tomorrow morning.'

Trying not to mind about the persistent use of 'we', Helen said carefully, 'Well, I'm glad you had an uneventful flight.'

'Yes, it wasn't too bad. And, Helen. . .?'

'Yes?'

'Sorry I snapped at you this morning.'

'That's all right.'

'It's just that. . . Well, you know there have been cases here in the United States of health workers or prison guards contracting TB through contact with patients or inmates, and I got a fright seeing you putting yourself at risk like that.'

'I understand, Nick.' That was all she had needed— a small apology and a tone which told her that he was no longer angry. She went on, 'I had a good talk with him afterwards. He's an interesting man, but I think I'm starting to understand his non-compliance. I think it's—'

'Oh-oh,' Nick interrupted. 'That's the door. Someone to replace a blown light-bulb. I'd better get it. Do you want me to ring you back?'

It was tempting to say, yes, but very unnecessary.

Helen said sensibly, 'No, don't bother. You're busy. Give me another ring in a few days.'

'All right, darling.'

Seconds later, the thin wire connection between them was cut, the house was silent again and Helen wondered why she had spent the whole day feeling desperate to hear his voice. To key herself up like that for just a few minutes of casual conversation! And she should be pleased that he had sounded so cheerful and relaxed, not resenting him because he didn't sound as if he was missing her! Angry with herself once again, Helen went to bed early.

Nick phoned three more times during the week. The first time it was just a brief, fairly practical chat and she couldn't help wanting more, although she knew that this didn't make sense. He sounded as warm as a husband should. After twenty years of marriage, was he going to mouth fervent love poems down the phone?

'We goofed off this afternoon,' he began.

'Goofed what?'

'Goofed off. I'm learning the language. There was a break from sessions and they'd organised some sightseeing for those who didn't want to play golf.' Nick politely and privately despised golf. . .perhaps because he wasn't any good at it! 'Weather was very nice and so it was a walking tour round the old part of the city. Could have been dull as ditchwater, but the guide was excellent. We stopped in at an old pub and were so late back we almost missed dinner.'

'We' being himself and Megan, or a whole group? Helen couldn't help wondering. She managed to resist the temptation to ask.

'Now, Helen, pearl of a thousand pearls, wife above all wives. . .?' Nick was saying.

'Yes?' she replied ominously, recognising this well-worn opening gambit for what it was. 'What do I have to do?'

'I don't know what the woman can possibly mean!' A bemused, helpless aside to his non-existent audience.

'The favour you're about to ask. Get to the point!' she scolded. 'It has to be done within the next half-hour, I suppose?'

'Well. . .' he admitted. 'Yesterday would have been even better, but tomorrow will do. I need an old paper of mine faxed over. Someone at the conference wants it, and I can't get hold of a copy here. Go to my desk, and look in the. . .'

She scribbled down his instructions, then snorted fondly at his idiotically humble gratitude. 'You know, after all these years of rubies beyond compare, diamonds of the first water, and all the costly perfumes of the mystic Orient that I've been promised in return for doing these errands for you. . .I've yet to see so much as a garnet or a pot of musk, I'll have you know!'

'I know. Honestly, this isn't too much of a nuisance, is it?'

'Of course it isn't! I'll swim the Atlantic personally if the hospital fax machine is out of order, with the papers clutched in my teeth.'

'Would you? Good, because I don't have a lot of confidence in that fax machine. And there's a rubber tyre tube in the garage that might buoy you up a bit. . .'

'Idiot. . .!'

His next call came on Friday night, just after the successful session built around his own paper, and the last one was on Sunday night, confirming his arrival time back at Manchester early on Monday morning. Wonderful! But was she imagining the coolness and reserve in his tone this time, in contrast to the other day?

'Do—do you want me to take the morning off and come to the airport?' she asked with timid hope.

'No, no, for heaven's sake! You'd have to get up at about five in the morning to get there in time. Megan will drive me back, since she's had her car ticking away in the long-stay car park all week at great expense. Nice to get home. It's been exhausting. We've got. . .some talking to do, too.'

Helen couldn't wait and, as she had done with his phone call last week, she keyed herself up to it at work all the following day, longing for him in any spare moments as she ran her single mothers' group, then drove her car from home visit to home visit and called in at two schools to administer standard TB skin tests.

Late in the afternoon she made another visit to tiny Rebecca Minty and her mother in the neonatal intensive care unit, and was able to catch Freda Minty awake, as she hadn't succeeded in doing last week. 'She's put on a bit of weight.'

'Yes,' the new mother said, standing by baby Rebecca's humidicrib and staring in at the tiny scrap of life on the white sheeting. 'Fifteen grams since yesterday. But, then, she lost ten grams a couple of days ago. Sometimes I feel if I so much as blow on the scales when they're weighing her I change the numbers and it's all meaningless. She's still tiny. If I glimpse another baby now it looks bloated to me, and that's wrong, isn't it?'

'That'll change as Rebecca herself starts to grow,' Helen soothed. She could see how frazzled and exhausted Mrs Minty looked and said, 'I talked to your mum and to the handicapped-access bus people, and they're going to add her to their route on Tuesdays and Thursdays. She's very pleased that she'll be able to get in here so easily now. Have you talked to her about it?'

'Oh. . . Yes. . . She's looking forward to it,' Freda Minty said vaguely. 'Look, I think she's waking up.'

'It'll mean you can take a bit of a break,' Helen prompted carefully. 'Is there anything special you'd like to do? Perhaps a gentle post-partum exercise class? I could arrange one for you. . .'

But the mother shook her head. 'No, I'll just stay here with Mum. She wouldn't want me to leave.'

It wasn't clear whether 'she' was baby Rebecca or elderly Mrs Shaw, but in either case it defeated the point of Mrs Shaw coming in. Helen didn't push the issue for today, but decided to enlist Peg Shaw's support instead in getting her daughter to take care of her own needs a little more.

The working day was nearly over. Helen had washed and styled her hair with extra care this morning and had put on her favourite work outfit—a softly draped blouse and skirt in a rich blue that set off her hair and eyes. She'd left a chicken and almond casserole in the fridge, too, as well as a supermarket apple pie in the freezer, all ready to pop into the oven as soon as she got home. There would be no repeat of last Monday's chaos in the kitchen to get in the way of their reunion.

But when she eagerly entered the house that evening it was as silent as it had been all last week, and there was only a roughly scrawled note from him on the kitchen table. 'Gone in to work. Back for dinner. Nick.' It sounded blunt, didn't it? It *did*! No 'love' before his name. None of his usual dry humour. But perhaps there was something urgent he had to see to and, after all, he was tired.

As Helen was. Somehow she hadn't been sleeping well all week, alone in the bed. She'd missed the warmth of Nick's strong back, pressed against hers, and the soft rhythm of his breathing.

He came at last—when the casserole was bubbling to perfection, the rice was done and the salad tossed. She heard his car in the drive and couldn't help running out, cannoning into him as he came around a lilac bush and almost diving into his arms, she was so eager for his touch. He held her, saying nothing, and they stood like that for a full minute until he released her and started into the house.

He still hadn't spoken until, 'Dinner smells good.'

'It's that casserole you like.'

'Ready now?'

'Yes. I'll serve, shall I?'

She hoped that he would come into the kitchen and help, as he so often did, but instead he had already disappeared into the study and didn't emerge until dinner was on the table. She had even opened a bottle of white wine, but when she held out the glass and the chilled bottle he shook his head with a frown. She felt foolish drinking alone in celebration of a reunion that he clearly didn't think was anything special, so she only poured herself the smallest half-glass and the wine sat there on the table between them, mocking her efforts.

We're not talking, she realised, as they both began to eat. Have we nothing to say to each other any more? Surely not! I'd hear every detail of his trip if he wanted to tell me. Is he waiting for me to ask?

He must be. She looked at him as he piled chicken and rice neatly onto the back of his fork. He was still frowning and staring down.

'Is there something—'

'I should tell you—'

They each began at the same moment, and stopped. 'You go,' he said.

'No, no. . .'

'Please.'

'I was just going to ask if there was something wrong. You seem. . .' distant, she wanted to say, but rejected the word and chose instead '. . .preoccupied.'

He sighed, stifled it and then said abruptly, 'MSUH definitely wants me. And Megan. To start in January.'

'But that's wonderful news, Nick!'

'Is it?' He frowned once more, and Helen's fingers suddenly itched to smooth out those heavy pleats in his brow and make his face as smooth and carefree as she knew it could be.

'Of course it is! It's a marvellous opportunity for you.' She was eager and smiling. 'I know how much you've wanted it, although you haven't really said.' She took a mouthful of the savoury casserole, then noticed that he had put down his own fork.

'I'm going to get some water, do you mind?' he said. 'My throat still feels dry from the plane. Back in a minute.'

He went into the kitchen, and she heard him getting out a glass and running the tap. Not strange behaviour, and yet he *was* behaving strangely tonight. He was! And she couldn't put her finger on it. He was back, beginning to speak before he had entered the room, his tone oddly careful and controlled. 'I admit I made the initial assumption that of course you'd come, but then I started thinking about it—trying to—from your perspective. There's the house and garden. Your job. The children. Pushcart.'

He still wasn't meeting her eye and his tone was so odd that Helen studied him closely, her heart suddenly beating faster. He was leading up to something with that list of his. 'After all, it is only for a year. I'd be able to get back two or three times to visit. If you wanted me to.'

'If I *wanted* you to?'

He responded stiffly to her high-pitched exclamation. 'I thought you might not feel it was. . .necessary.'

'Necessary? But you're saying—' She broke off as she suddenly realised what he meant, then continued in a wooden tone, 'If I stayed behind.'

There! It was out. He wasn't denying it and she knew from his expression that this was the thing that had been in the air between them ever since that last stilted call from Boston. He was going to work at MSUH for a year, and she was to stay behind in England. He had offered some undeniably practical reasons. The children. Yes, it would be a hideous wrench to be so far from Jon and Jane. Her job, too. She would probably have to resign.

And perhaps if he had just offered those two impediments she might have thought that he was expressing a sincere concern. They could have discussed it. Would she really mind so much about resigning? And couldn't they both come back to visit Jon and Jane, or fly them over to Boston in the summer break?

The house and garden, too, were legitimate concerns. For that length of time, they would have to try and get a tenant. But mentioning the cat? Dear old Pushcart, who didn't care what went on as long as she was fed and could come and go through her cat-door? That was protesting too much!

He doesn't want me to go. He's finding excuses to convince me to stay behind. . .

'Yes, I see. . . Look, I'd better check on the pie,' she managed, and fled into the kitchen, trying not to hurry so that he wouldn't suspect that she was leaving the room to hide her threatened tears.

When the possibility of this year in Boston had first arisen he had said nothing about this idea. Nothing! Neither of them had said much, in fact, but surely in both their minds had been the idea that, once it was definite, they would talk over the practicalities. In fact, he had said as much over dinner the night before he left.

I thought he'd be worried about me being bored, she realised. *I was going to tell him how much I was looking forward to having some time to myself, and some time to spend on him.*

Actually, her fantasies about the year in Boston were quite well formed. She would have the leisure at last to plan weekends away for the two of them, exploring the New England region, and time to cook for him without the chaos which so often ensued as she dashed straight into the kitchen after work. She could take up a craft. American quilting, perhaps. Or a sport. Ice-skating! A sport *and* a craft! And when Nick came home at the end of a tiring day he wouldn't find an equally exhausted and even more frazzled wife, but a relaxed, well-groomed creature who could soothe away his fatigue with sheer, unadulterated cosseting.

She had already started to see it as the best year of their marriage, and yet now he was telling her very carefully, very sensibly, and without meeting her eye once, that she wasn't to go to Boston with him at all. She was to stay at home and look after Pushcart!

Shakily she made a pretence of checking on the pie, opening the squeaky oven door. Yes, yes, it looked more or less done. All appetite had fled and she didn't care at the moment if it was still—being the supermarket variety—frozen solid in the middle. She turned off the oven.

Nick didn't want her to go. He hadn't wanted her to go to the conference last week either, but this was different, wasn't it? She had agreed with him that for six days it wasn't worth it, and with Jon and Jane at such an important point in their lives. . . Only now she started to wonder. Were those just excuses as well, very convenient ones because she happened to agree with them? What was the real reason, then?

She didn't need to search far to find the answer. Megan Stone.

Oh, God, Stella Harris would think I was crazy. I've just let my husband spend six nights alone in a five-star hotel with a beautiful and intelligent woman whom I suspect is in love with him! *Is* he having an affair with her? Not my Nick! He can't be. Megan wants it, I'm sure of it, but *he* doesn't. A man is vulnerable when he's away, though, isn't he? No, *not* my Nick!

She would have had him into her room for a drink after dinner to talk about the conference sessions. He might not have intended anything to happen but when it did. . .he found that there was a whole lot igniting between them that's been missing in our marriage lately. Should I confront him with it? We can talk and I'll forgive it and he'll swear it won't happen again. No! It *didn't* happen at all! *Not my Nick!*

The thoughts went round and round, and she was miserable. She had been gone for far longer than it took to simply check a pie, yet he hadn't called out to see what was the matter—which, in itself, was odd and wrong. She pulled herself together, intending to go back out to him and talk. Surely if they talked. . .? They *had* to talk! And yet the more she said this to herself the more the words dammed themselves up against some blockage in her throat, and she knew that anything she said would come out all wrong—as it had done when she'd tried to talk to Jane about that foolish engagement.

If she angrily accused him of having an affair and he denied it, she would feel as if a reasonless jealousy within her had broken down their bonds of trust. And if he admitted it. . . The thought of hearing Nick say those words, 'I'm sorry, Helen, I think I'm falling in love with Megan. It's not your fault. . .' Because, even in the midst of her worst fear, she knew he would be kind about it. 'I didn't want to. It just happened. I'm sorry.'

Her sympathy for bitter Stella suddenly increased tenfold. How did a wife survive that pain and betrayal? Yet women *did* have to survive it all the time these days. And she realised for the first time that she shared an arrogant presumption with the other married women at her work when they thought of Stella—thank God it could never happen to me!

But perhaps it could.

I'm being ridiculous. Her legs were so weak now that she was having to lean against the kitchen bench, but still Nick didn't come to find out what was wrong. And he didn't want her to go to Boston with him, trying to disguise the fact as concern for the damned cat! Aside from everything else that could just be her tortured imagination, this fact stood out clearly and could not be denied.

Still weak and shaky, she got herself a glass of water

and went back to the dining-room with not a clue as to what she was going to say.

It was funny how you could live under the same roof—outwardly amicable, chatting about day-to-day things, even making love occasionally—and still not really be connected or in communication at all. In the end she had said nothing to Nick that night about what she was feeling, and the subject of Boston had been quietly dropped as if he, too, was reluctant to say any more.

Over a week went by and, increasingly, they were like polite strangers. No, not like strangers, more like work colleagues who had known each other for a long time and couldn't stand each other but who preserved a front of almost treacly cordiality because they knew that they had to co-exist.

In the many silences between them—over breakfast, or in the evenings with a backdrop of television—words crowded onto Helen's tongue and burned there, remaining always unspoken. She did make some attempts to open up the subject but they were so ineffectual that Nick always deflected them, whether deliberately or by chance she still could not decide.

'So, if you and Megan are both in Boston, what's going to happen to thoracic medicine at Camberton?' was one such attempt, over breakfast on Thursday.

His response was practical and to the point. 'Tony Glover will head up the department, and we'll appoint a new consultant. Not Megan, after all, obviously, because she'd rather come to Boston. And then there'll be a direct exchange with someone from MSUH, Nathan Fleischman. He's good. I expect. . . Well, I'm sure you'll get to meet him. There's a lot to do to get it all organised. I'm going to be run off my feet for the next few months.'

'Megan would rather go to Boston than work towards her consultancy?'

'At this stage, yes. She's got plenty of time. And, with the experience she gets at MSUH, she'll be able to go anywhere she likes once she does become a consultant.'

'So it's all working out well for everyone.'

'Yes.' His tone was rather stiff. 'It would appear so.'

And that was that. Helen realised that if she couldn't broach the subject directly nothing would ever get said, yet still those bald phrases stuck in her mouth. Why don't you want me with you? Is this the first step towards separation and divorce? Are you in love with Megan?

Meanwhile, their working lives went on. Nick felt that Agatha Miller was ready for discharge, and brought the weight of his own authority to bear on the matter of the 'little whiffs'—to the point where elderly Mrs Miller was round-eyed and reverent and seemed to believe that she might die tomorrow if she didn't have her nasal tube or venturi mask in place at all times.

Barbara James, struggling to establish rules and routines in her newly expanded household, was very grateful for this—if a little amused at her wilful mother's sudden quiescence.

Helen paid a visit to the Jameses' house on Friday morning, arriving earlier than she had expected to, and at first it seemed that no one was home. The car was gone from the open garage and no one answered the front doorbell. Slightly alarmed, she followed a rhythmic sound coming from the back and found Agatha, sitting in a wicker armchair on the back porch, just as her daughter had predicted, smoking contentedly with her nasal tube feeding her oxygen while she sucked in tar and nicotine through her mouth. She was tapping her chunky black heels on the porch floor, which made the sound that had caught Helen's attention.

She looked guilty as soon as she saw Helen. 'Just once in a while isn't going to hurt,' she said defensively. 'And what're you doing coming round the back, anyway?'

'No one answered the bell. I was worried about you.'

'Nosey one, she is,' the old woman muttered to the air, and Helen pretended not to hear.

Covertly, she counted the cigarettes left in the open packet on Mrs Miller's lap so that she'd be able to ask Barbara if she knew when the packet had been full. Just five left, and it was a packet of twenty. Mrs Miller had only come home from the hospital on Wednesday, two days ago. If it had been a new packet then, she was smoking at least fifteen a day—which made a mockery of her hospital therapy.

'How long will your daughter be, Mrs Miller?' Helen asked.

'Well, she's gone to get Geoffrey from nursery school, but then she had to pop up to the shops. Couldn't tell you, really.'

'Perhaps I'd better try another time, then.'

'Eh, if you like. 'S not my business.'

Helen left, swallowing the sense—which some home visits could give her—that she was invading privacy in her professional role. Once again she thought of the emphysema support group. Perhaps someone like Mrs Miller would respond better to suggestions about her health made in a group situation. She had planned to talk the idea of the support group over with Nick, but the intangible gulf widening so unexpectedly between them had distracted her and put her off and she hadn't done it.

'Dr Snaith would be interested too,' she decided on a sigh as she drove away from the Jameses' house. 'Perhaps I'll discuss my suggestion with him instead.'

She would be seeing Dr Snaith up at the hospital this afternoon. For that matter, she would be seeing Nick, too. They were due to meet, together with Megan Stone, Karen Graham, some other professionals and no doubt a sizeable contingent of medical students, for a case conference in the chest ward's conference room to discuss Paul Chambers and the issue of his treatment and discharge.

Over her sandwich lunch Helen typed up some ideas

about the support group, then drove up to Camberton Hospital for the case conference. The watery sunshine that Agatha Miller had enjoyed this morning was gone now, and the sky was opening up in scattered showers, with scarves of grey cloud draping the hills around the small city. Narrowly missing a drenching, Helen parked in the visitors' car park and went inside to find that she was a little early and that no one had gathered yet.

'Would you like some tea?' Karen Graham offered.

'I'd love some! But I'll do it,' Helen added, seeing that the ward sister was struggling to complete some notes before she was required at the case conference. 'How is Mr Chambers, by the way?'

'Prowling. Grumpy. Go and see him,' Karen suggested, so Helen left her tea drawing and did so, taking the particulate respirator Nick now required health care staff to wear whenever they were in the infectious man's room.

'Hi.' It was awkward having to talk to him like this, and the respirator distorted her voice.

He glowered at her. 'God, you all look like idiots wearing those things!'

'Yes, I expect we do,' she agreed calmly. 'Perhaps we should be photographed, and you can put us up on the wall in a collage and throw darts at us.'

He gave a bark of unwilling laughter and his ferocious brow cleared a little.

'I think you've put on a bit of weight,' Helen went on, but this time he glared again.

'Half a kilo. You can't possibly tell me it shows!'

'I cheated,' she admitted. 'I looked at your chart. But any weight gain is a good sign, and you *do* look better.'

'Feel it,' he acknowledged grudgingly. 'Appetite's come back a bit. Although these drugs are crucifying my liver.'

'Have you told the dietician?'

'Yes, and according to your goodly spouse I must

not imbibe alcohol until further notice or I'll turn bright yellow. He also claims that I have a few billion less bacilli in my lungs, according to my cultures—but I have to take his word on that one.'

'The bacilli are responding to treatment. Shouldn't you be pleased about that?' Her voice sounded both muffled and echoey to her own ears as it came through the respirator.

'Probably,' he conceded. 'However, I find I rarely react the way I should when it comes to my disease. The very fact that I have some sincere, starchy creature observing my every move as I take enough pills to kill a horse, for example, has of late engendered a surprisingly physical resistance to swallowing. I simply can't get the damn things down, and if I chew them they taste so vile that I gag. They're all out there by the desk at pill-time, drawing straws to see who gets stuck with the grisly task of watching me. Can't wait till I get home and can take them in private.'

'That's not going to happen, Mr Chambers,' Helen told him bluntly.

'What? No! You're wrong! They're talking about discharge if my cultures look good in a couple of weeks. There's some confab about it today.'

'Yes, I know,' she came in quickly. 'Sorry, I explained badly.' And he was clearly shaken, she could see, at the thought of having to stay here indefinitely. 'I meant that when you *are* discharged you won't be able to take your pills in private. My husband is going to want you under directly observed therapy if you're going to go home.'

'Well, I won't do it! What? Some woman wearing support stockings made of beige concrete comes round on a bicycle and leers at me with a hairy upper lip until I get them down?'

'Actually, it'll probably be me and, anyway, that gorgon-on-a-bicycle stereotype is way out of date.'

'You? Hmm. . .' he growled, then studied her—or

what he could see of her beyond the particulate respirator. 'That's a slightly more bearable concept.' She felt herself blushing at his flagrant regard. 'But you must have days off. . .?'

'There's a district nurse, part-time—Sally Lawton.'

'Or perhaps I could persuade my darling Karen to minister to me in her free time?'

'I doubt it,' Helen returned, alarmed by the salacious glint in his eye. 'She's busy with her boyfriend when she has time off.'

This was a pure fabrication but she felt protective, suddenly, towards the pretty blonde ward sister. She had no illusions about Paul Chambers, and knew that he would be capable of using and abusing the slightest nuance of personal interest that developed in conscientious Karen Graham.

Thinking of Karen, she realised that she had already spent too long with Paul Chambers. What was it about the man? He seemed to need to draw everyone into his orbit, and she didn't look forward to visiting him daily in his home to ensure that he complied with his treatment. Somehow he would exact an additional toll from her for it, she was certain.

In the ward conference room, breathing thankfully without the respirator once again, Helen was amongst the last to sit down, holding her cooling tea. In fact, everyone was here except Nick, and he strode in just as she had got out her diary and balanced it on her lap.

'Ah, good!' He looked somewhat harried, and his smile was just a sketch as his gaze skated over the gathered group and tallied up those present. His special acknowledgement of Helen was so brief as to be almost non-existent. 'Let's start, then. Dr Stone should be here shortly.' Of course! Megan's was the other missing face. Helen's heart sank and she was suddenly dreading the case conference, although there seemed no good reason for this.

'For those of you unfamiliar with the case,' Nick was saying, as he acknowledged the handful of earnestly white-coated medical students, 'I'll give you a full background.'

And now everyone focused fully. Helen sat back in her chair and watched him, so dynamic, so absorbed. His eyes scarcely ever dropped to his notes, and his gestures chopped the air boldly. 'Patient is a man of forty-four, freelance journalist, Paul Chambers. History of some alcohol abuse, though I wouldn't label him an alcoholic. Admits to some drug abuse, too—not intravenous—but says he stopped that some years ago as it began to seem "too adolescent". Ex-smoker, no previous serious illness of any kind. "Healthy as a horse." Again, those are his own words.'

There was a small commotion in the doorway and Nick stopped, looked up and smiled. Megan had entered, immaculate in a crimson suit and dramatically high-heeled shoes which would have had Helen's feet howling in protest by the end of half an hour. She saw two pairs of male medical students' eyes widen and flash in appreciation, and when Nick resumed his speech—after Megan had sat down beside him with a murmured apology—wasn't there more animation to him and a rich tone in his voice that hadn't been there before? No, of course not!

Nick's detailed summary went on as he described how Paul Chambers had contracted the disease, what had led to the fear that it was a multi-drug-resistant strain and what the resulting treatment strategy had been. 'By getting as detailed a history as we could and sending some extensive—and expensive—faxes to New York, we managed to pin down the most likely strain as being one that is resistant to two of the first-line antibiotics but, fortunately, not the other three. Perhaps you could tell us what all five of those drugs are, Mr Stewart?'

He flashed the unexpected question at one of the medical students, who had been gazing at Megan from beneath a thick fringe of straight brown hair. Helen stifled a smile. There had been nothing threatening in Nick's manner, but the student flushed and stuttered all the same and didn't dare to look at the senior registrar again. If the latter had been aware of either the looking or the avoidance, she gave no sign.

'Um. . . Well, let's see. . .' He stumbled through the five multisyllabic names and reached the end of the list with visible relief.

Nick had nodded at each one. 'Yes, good. Not hard. Most of those first-line antibiotics have been in standard use since the early nineteen-fifties. So, by adding two of the second-line drugs. . . Here, don't write it down. I've made a chart with the full projected treatment regimen.'

He handed out a sheet of paper to each student and Adam Stewart took one, then subsided into relieved anonymity once again. 'We hope, if we have indeed identified the particular strain correctly, to eliminate all living bacilli within. . .well, let's be optimistic. . .six months. But of course he'll be non-infectious far sooner than that, which is why it's appropriate to start thinking about discharge now. Straightforward, one would think. However. . .'

He began to detail the patient's past problem with compliance. 'So you see, we're not only dealing with a likely transmitted resistance here, but with an acquired resistance created by the patient's erratic self-treatment in the past. Doesn't fit the profile for that, does he? He's not homeless, mentally ill, poorly educated, intellectually impaired, chronically alcoholic or drug dependent—all of which can be psychological or socio-economic indicators signalling the possibility of poor compliance. So, what's the problem here? Why is he unreliable?

'Helen, you might like to comment on that. I think you're one of the people who has spent the most time actually in conversation with him. Are there any insights you've gained that may throw some light on this?'

She started and gaped a little, feeling as nakedly spot-lighted as Adam Stewart had been some minutes ago. Nick had turned to her, her name liquid and at the same time quite short on his lips. He was watching her, waiting, every inch the professional as he flexed his tired shoulders for a moment. No one would have guessed that they were married. She gathered her thoughts quickly, determined not to be needlessly self-conscious under his scrutiny, and then caught the familiar twinkle of humour in his grey eyes that she loved so much. It gave her the focus she needed.

'Yes, I think I do have some insights. Mr Chambers has a strong sense of his own invincibility,' she began carefully and clearly, 'coupled with a need to romanticise himself, by placing himself at the centre of dramatic situations and then recording those situations in detail with the aim of creating a fairly hard-hitting, sensational kind of journalism. To put it another way, he thinks that his own flirtatious dance with death will make a good book and still hasn't fully accepted that it might be death itself that ultimately calls the tune, not him.'

She stopped, saw how surprised Nick looked and realised that she hadn't actually told him this before—and certainly not in the form of the dramatic metaphor she had just used.

'Strong stuff,' he said, sitting back a little, and for a moment she wondered whether she had overstated the case—put it too bluntly and vividly in her attempt to be clear and hold the interest of the group. Remembering her exchanges with the man, though, she knew that she hadn't.

Megan was frowning, and looking hesitantly sceptical. 'If I could come in here,' she murmured with an oddly tentative smile.

'Of course, Megan.' Nick leaned forward encouragingly.

'I see it slightly differently. As Helen says, it's the man's profession as a journalist that is at the heart of the problem, but I would say it was a more prosaic one than she allows. He's a busy man and, yes, he has an inflated sense of his own dramatic importance. This led, during his first treatment, to a false belief that he was cured. He now realises that this was premature and, in the talks I've had with him, I've come to believe that he will now take full responsibility for his own treatment once he's discharged.'

On the far side of the room Helen saw that Karen Graham had gone pink-cheeked, her mouth was opened in protest and her blue eyes glittered anxiously.

Nick, not in a good position to see everyone, hadn't noticed. 'OK, so we have two opinions on this. That needs to be noted, as it will influence our decision about when and *whether* to discharge. At the moment there's still no question of it. Indications are that his disease is responding to the treatment we've been giving him, but until we get a satisfactory sputum culture and can isolate the exact strain and the drugs it's resistant to we'll have to keep him here. I'm inclined to support—'

He broke off as he looked from Helen to Megan and back again, then went on decisively after a moment, 'No, at this stage, I can't support one or other theory about his past non-compliance and whether it's likely to continue.'

Helen saw Karen Graham shift in her seat again, and came in quickly, 'I think Karen has something to add to that issue.'

But the pink-cheeked ward sister shook her head energetically at Nick's raised eyebrows and Helen was a little embarrassed at having singled out the other nurse. She was sure that Karen had something to say. Was she embarrassed about speaking to a group? Why should that be?

Helen felt uncomfortable, as well, about not having gained Nick's automatic support for her ideas about Paul

Chambers, as opposed to Megan's. It was rare for there to be any awkwardness in the fact that their work brought them together professionally at times. And it *isn't* awkward now, she told herself firmly. Of course he can't automatically agree with my analysis just because I'm his wife.

But a small, angry voice inside her offered a different opinion. His love for her ought to include respect for her judgement. It always had before. The way he had looked between the two of them just then—Helen across the room on his right, Megan directly at his left—had really emphasised the fact that he would have to choose between Megan's ideas and her own, and suddenly that seemed horribly significant—as if very soon he might be making a far more meaningful choice than that.

The case conference continued with discussion from Dr Snaith and one of the hospital's social workers, then Helen and the other professionals left, while Nick, Megan, two junior doctors and the medical students remained for an in-depth teaching session about tuberculosis in the 1990s before actually going in to see the patient.

Helen stopped at the nurses' station on her way out. 'Did you have something on your mind, Karen?'

'Oh. . .' The shrug was noncommittal.

'I thought perhaps you didn't want to speak in front of a large group, but I could mention it to Nick for you if there is something.'

'Well, it's not so much that.' The ward sister was blushing again, then she lifted her chin in a gesture of defiance. 'Actually, I think you and Dr Stone are both wrong in what you've decided about Paul. He *will* go on having trouble keeping to his treatment once he's discharged, but not because he thinks he's immune to death. He's just. . .not the sort of man who lives on that plane. When he's working he just forgets about everything—forgets to eat, forgets to sleep. He needs. . .well, a wife, really, except that he doesn't believe in actual marriage. He needs a woman who cares about him enough to do all that for him. That's all.'

'And *is* there a woman?'

'No. There isn't. Not at the moment.'

The words and the tone were so intensely significant that Helen could only blurt it aloud without thinking of tact, 'No, Karen! Not *you*!'

'No. He's a patient. I can't and won't,' was Karen Graham's low, fierce reply. 'But once he's discharged, if he wants me. . .'

'And does he?'

'He must.' Her colour was hectic. 'What I feel is already so strong I know he has to return it, although he's too scrupulous to compromise me professionally by saying so directly. Oh, but the way he—'

The phone on her desk rang at that moment and she snatched it up impatiently. Helen was too disturbed to say anything more, and knew that, in any case, she was scarcely in a position to give warnings or advice. Nick didn't seem to feel that she had the right to try to influence even her own daughter in affairs of the heart. As for a casual professional acquaintance. . .

But Karen's burgeoning feelings were an alarming development in what was already a dramatic case, and Helen was very glad about the upcoming weekend and the opportunity to relax away from work. Last weekend Nick had been too busy catching up on things after the Boston conference, and had scarcely set foot in the house on either day, but this weekend it should be different.

There'll be a chance to talk at last, Helen promised herself. And this time I won't let myself be put off.

Driving together in the car, perhaps. They had a dinner party tomorrow night at the house of some old friends connected with Camberton Hospital, and then on Sunday they were travelling to a little village near Sheffield for afternoon tea with another long-known couple. Liz

Holloway was pregnant for the first time at thirty-seven, after a long battle with infertility, and her twins were due very soon.

We still haven't made the time to get our anniversary china, but it'll be so good to see friends. We'll both be feeling more at ease. Just the right time to get rid of all these silly fears. . .

She left the chest ward after a brief, distracted goodbye to Karen, whose fierce blush was only just subsiding, and then met Dr Snaith on his way out too. Remembering the ideas she had typed up about her proposed emphysema support group, Helen broached the subject in the lift and by the time they reached the doctors' car park Stephen Snaith's boyish face was alive with enthusiasm.

'Nick must like the idea.'

'Actually, I haven't talked to him about it yet.'

'You haven't? But you must!'

'Oh, I know. I must, and I will talk to him. This weekend,' Helen replied, thinking of the wider meaning of her words, and the young doctor frowned slightly at the note of fervency in her voice.

Home visits made up the rest of Helen's afternoon. She set one mother straight on the correct treatment for mild burns—*not* butter or petroleum jelly, but a lengthy plunge of the affected area into cold water as soon after the accident as possible. Another was worried about her child's eyesight, and they arranged for a check-up in case glasses were needed.

A third family, whose three children were on Camberton's alert list for possible non-accidental injuries, had some good news to report—the father had a job at last. 'In a garage!' Lee-Anne Shoemaker said. 'He's always loved tinkering with cars, and if he does well he might end up a qualified mechanic. He's that pleased about it! He's been gentle as a lamb all week.' She added hastily, 'Not that he's rough, really. . . It was the unemployment got him down.' Knowing a fair bit about the family by this time, Helen thought there was a good chance that Mrs Shoemaker was right and that things would improve from now on.

Back at the health centre, she caught up her mileage log, tidied her desk and, in an act of pure altruism, searched out all the dirty coffee-cups that irresponsible doctors had left lying about during the day! She arrived home in time to cook, and made a veal and sage stew with baked potatoes, carrots and broccoli, hoping that Nick wouldn't arrive until it was aromatic and ready to serve. Once it *was* ready, however, and he still wasn't home she was impatient and restless, and listened constantly for his car in the drive, not able to concentrate on anything else.

He came at last, at a quarter past seven, his clothes giving off a strong odour of cigarette smoke. 'Sorry. . .' Rather stiff. 'I did try to ring, but you weren't home yet. We really must get a machine.'

'I've been home since half past five,' she said, and of course it came out like an accusation. It *was* one!

'I know, I should have tried to ring again, but well. . .I got caught up.'

'In what?'

'Megan asked some of us out for a drink. Tony Glover, Callum Priestley. She had a book review accepted in one of the American medical journals, and she was celebrating.'

'Well, dinner's been ready since a quarter to seven. . .' Oh, Helen, get a grip on yourself! She sounded like a martyred doormat. If things hadn't been so odd and wrong lately, she would have been happy that he'd enjoyed a drink to unwind on a Friday night. He certainly deserved it, and she'd done the same thing with her own colleagues on occasion.

And if things hadn't been so odd and wrong lately, he might have tried to tease her out of her pique. As it was he said, stiffer than ever, 'I did apologise. I'll apologise again. I'm sorry. Next time I won't go.'

'No!' she came in contritely. 'I didn't mean that!'

They both tried over dinner to patch things up, avoiding subjects of any real importance in their talk. Then Nick made a long phone call to a colleague in Boston, where it was still only three in the afternoon, while Helen cleared up and then sat at the desk in the sitting-room, writing out cheques for bills. The house was very quiet and she put on some classical music, thinking, Jon will groan, then remembering, No, he's in London now.

As usual she was in bed a little before Nick, but she was still awake when he came.

'Restless?' he asked.

'Not really. You know it always takes me a little while to drop off.'

'Got something that might help. . .'

And a moment later he reached out for her gently. She wore a soft, full nightdress of cotton lawn tonight, not particularly sexy but pretty and nice, and it was fine enough to transmit the warmth of his touch instantly through to her skin. Those soft, caressing strokes that she loved; the feel of him nuzzling her hair and neck and cheek. She began to tingle and swell. . .wanting him, wanting to be lost in him. . .

But then she was angry. It couldn't be like this! Not talking, not connecting—then pretending that it didn't matter when he wanted to make love. Never mind that she wanted it too! She willed her body's response away, tightened her limbs then said, not turning to him, 'Not tonight, if you don't mind.' No explanation, just that.

His caresses stopped. His hand stayed where it was for a moment, then withdrew. 'That's all right,' she heard, and then he rolled over, not pressing the length of his back against hers as he so often did—so that they warmed and supported each other—but moving right away, leaving six inches of cold sheet between them.

Helen churned with regret. In twenty years of marriage

she had gently turned aside his male needs before, of course, but only out of real fatigue or illness or mental preoccupation. Until tonight, until just now, she'd never refused his love-making out of a desire to punish him—out of pique or anger. What an unfelicitous 'first'!

She was miserable about it and almost turned to him in remorse, but then she found that she was crying instead, silent tears that she absolutely had to keep to herself. When they subsided she listened and heard the sound of regular breathing that told her he was asleep. Asleep. . .or pretending very well. Quietly she slipped out of bed, went into the kitchen and made herself some cocoa, then sat at the table drinking it for quite a long time.

CHAPTER FIVE

'Hmm, I thought this was going to be a *small* dinner party,' Nick murmured as he turned into the curved gravel driveway of the Wymans' house and saw the cars that filled the three available parking spaces. The four cars they had noticed parked in the street out the front clearly belonged to the dinner guests, too, and the Darnells' own modest sedan was forced to join the line a little further along.

'Do you mind?' Helen said.

'A bit. I was looking forward to some quiet, civilised conversation over a sit-down meal. These cars are saying "buffet" to me, loud and clear.'

She laughed. 'Looks that way. But you're so good at circulating.'

'Thanks,' he responded with a self-mocking grin. 'Doesn't mean I like it!'

They parked and walked up the drive, Helen's heels bogging down in the deep gravel so that Nick had to take her arm. Not an unwelcome gesture, by any means. She snuggled against him, then felt him stiffen and stop in his tracks. 'What's the——?' she began.

'Listen, Helen. This is no good. We have to have a proper talk.'

'I know,' she said, suddenly miserable.

He had been out for most of the day, dealing with two emergency admissions—one with pulmonary embolism, the other with acute oxygen deprivation due to a spinal condition called scoliosis—and then a crisis in the health of one of his long-term cystic fibrosis patients.

Helen had shopped and cleaned and done laundry, reconciled to the mundane nature of the day by the promise of tonight's outing and tomorrow's drive and tea. She had already begun dressing before he returned home, and there had been a kind of closeness and truce—except that that word made them sound like enemies, which they weren't, surely—as he'd showered and shaved while she put on her make-up and jewellery.

She loved listening to the healthy way he splashed under the water. He didn't actually go so far as to sing but he was certainly exuberant, and when he'd bounded out in search of a fresh towel, water dripping down his hair-darkened chest and glistening on the smooth lines of his shoulders and hips, she could easily have forgotten all about going out and just wrestled him onto the bed. She hadn't, though, afraid that it would have brought up last night and her rebuff of him.

The ten-minute drive to the Wymans' had been pleasant, however, with light, friendly conversation which had given her some confidence that she'd be able to talk about deeper things on the longer drive tomorrow. Now, though, it seemed that what they had said to each other in the car had just been papering over the cracks and the distance between them was back, more evident than ever in the way he had stiffened at her gesture of intimacy as she walked beside him.

She knew what *she* wanted to talk about. Her fears about their marriage; her sense that he wasn't supporting her over Jane and that disastrous engagement, Boston. . . She wanted to say, 'Please take me with you! Surely, if we're away together, we can work at what's gone wrong and sort it out. Do you really want to let it all go without a fight?'

But what did *he* have to say? His brooding, dissatisfied face, lit from one side by the bluish light on the Wymans' porch, frightened and dismayed her. He was giving so little away.

'Since it *is* a party, not a small dinner,' Nick was saying now, 'do you think they'd mind if we ducked out and came back in half an hour—?'

He broke off. Another couple was coming up the steps towards them. Richard Hartman was Chief of Surgery at Camberton Hospital and his wife, Nina, was a specialist in neonatal surgery and, of course, the Hartmans swept Nick and Helen inside with greetings and questions about the Boston conference and Jon and Jane.

'It'll have to wait,' Nick found time to say to Helen tightly. 'I was an idiot to think that this was the time. God, you'd think that living under the same roof we'd at least manage to—'

He didn't finish, having been seized by Derek Wyman—the hospital's medical administrator—who hadn't realised that Nick was even speaking, his aside had been so low and terse-lipped.

'Gaye is in the kitchen, Helen,' Derek said. 'Do go and see her because she's dying to catch up.' In another minute Derek and Nick were both on the far side of the room, getting drinks with the Hartmans, and Helen, left alone and still drinkless, dutifully made her way to the kitchen.

Gaye Wyman, an energetic part-time physiotherapist of forty-five, and a good friend, was frantically supervising her two young daughters in their assistance with the catering. She had been away with both of them for most of the summer, visiting her parents who had retired to the south of France. Naturally she wanted to hear Helen's news, and tell her own. And, naturally, since much evidently remained to be done before the meal was served, Helen stayed in the kitchen to help.

Right at this moment, Gaye didn't have time to talk about anything but her cooking. 'Here's a glass of wine, Helen. Now, if you could get those mushroom vol-au-vents out of the oven before they burn and put them on this tray with the shrimp toast, and take them round. . . Thanks! You're angelic! I'll pay you a pound an hour,' she finished drily.

'A pound an hour?'

'That's what the girls demanded. For the past hour, though, they *haven't* been earning it!' She frowned at Claire and Sarah, aged thirteen and eleven, who giggled and got solemn and attacked their fruit salad preparations with renewed vigour.

Helen arranged the piping hot vol-au-vents attractively, then went out to the guests who now crowded the open-plan dining and living areas. They were mainly hospital people. She knew most of them at least slightly, either through Nick or through her own work, and they smiled as they took her proffered hors d'oeuvres and stopped her for a phrase or two of conversation.

Callum Priestley—a senior registrar in cardiothoracic surgery—engaged her for a little longer, talking energetically in his robust Newcastle accent. He seemed to be here unaccompanied, and that was a great pity, she considered. Younger women had no sense, these days. . . Running after married men, while men like Callum still went unclaimed! A talented surgeon, he was an intensely ugly man, big and rough-cut in all his features. . .but so warm and interesting. . . Younger women—like Megan Stone, for example—must be so shallow not to see the worth beneath that forbidding countenance!

But she had to excuse herself to Callum after a few minutes as she couldn't let Gaye down by keeping these hors d'oeuvres out of circulation. No one else seemed to be helping. Nina Hartman certainly wasn't. A little too coldly brilliant to be likeable, she ran her own household with the help of a nanny, a full-time housekeeper and casual cleaners twice a week, and it probably didn't occur to her that Gaye and Derek were managing this big party with only the dubious help of two giggling daughters.

Helen put down the vol-au-vents and picked up a tray of biscuits and cheese in one hand, and dip and crisps in the other, and circulated with those as well. She passed Nick, and he took a couple absently, still talking to Nina, and she wondered angrily if either of them had even noticed who she was.

No, Nick must have. She looked back at him and found that his grey eyes were on her, but when he saw her own gaze he flicked his frowning attention quickly away. It was a very distancing gesture and now, once again, he was nodding at Nina Hartman's words. Helen's throat tightened more and more as the minutes passed. It almost seemed as if he was deliberately avoiding her.

And no one was touching the vol-au-vents unless prompted. She realised that it would make more sense to have Claire and Sarah out here playing waitresses while she lent her more experienced hands to Gaye in the kitchen. Gaye was grateful for the suggestion. 'If you really don't mind.'

'Not at all,' Helen assured her, then added abruptly, 'Actually, I'm not feeling very social tonight.'

'No?' Gaye was instantly sympathetic. 'I thought you looked a bit strained. Run down? Or missing the twins?'

'Well, that, of course.' Helen hesitated then plunged in, suddenly badly in need of a friend and a talk. 'Actually, it's Nick.'

'Nick?'

'Nick and me.' She stirred the soup erratically as she spoke. 'We're...we're... We don't seem to be getting on.'

'Not getting on?'

'Oh, Gaye, don't just parrot it back at me like that!' Helen burst out. 'Is it so impossible to understand?'

'Well, no, I understand it.' Gaye waved her hands in agitation, then clasped them beseechingly together. 'But...you and he always seem so good together. There are times when I've been quite envious. Are you saying that's just for show?'

'No! At least... No, I've always thought we *did* get on—until just lately. But now, with the twins gone, I wonder. Perhaps this has been happening for a while, only I've been too busy to notice, and it's only with Jon and Jane out on their own that it's been brought into focus.'

'That's it, of course,' Gaye said kindly. 'It's a time of transition for you. Things are bound to seem different, unsettling.'

'Yes, that would make sense, if that was all it was.' Helen added cream to the soup, aware of Gaye's intent expression during the short silence. Then she went on abruptly, 'But it's more. It's *not* me. It's Nick. Gaye, he's got this Boston stint for a year, starting in January, and he doesn't want me to go! He's latched onto some plausible excuses—like the twins and my job—but underneath he doesn't want me with him, and all I can assume is that it's a prelude to an even wider rift in the future.'

'My God, Helen, you're not talking about divorce?' Gaye was aghast.

Helen spread her hands, tear-blinded and unable to speak. She had said the word to herself often enough over the past week or two but this was the first time it had been spoken aloud and, far from assuaging her fears, Gaye's mixture of disbelief and sympathy was only making everything worse.

'But if it's just a matter of drifting apart,' she was saying now, 'surely you can work at it. I mean, there's no question of another woman or anything, is there? And—' She stopped, seeing Helen's stark expression. 'There *is* someone? Oh, no, *Helen*! *Who*?'

She managed to speak at last, although it came out as a hoarse whisper through her clenched throat. 'Megan Stone.' Then it all came tumbling out.

'And of course they've just been in Boston together and she's to go in January as well. It was when he arrived back from the conference that I knew I wasn't just imagining things. We hardly say a word to each other at home, and at the hospital Megan follows him with her eyes and has a love-struck smile on her face.

'She told me straight out that Nick and I were bucking the odds to be still together after twenty years, having married so young. It sounded like a wonderfully plausible rationale for our break-up. Not Nick's fault. Not mine. We've just grown in different directions and "one of us", that is, Nick, is going to find someone more compatible, that is, Megan, and. . .and. . . Thank God she isn't here tonight!'

Gaye made a face. 'She's supposed to be. She rang to say she was delayed at the hospital, and she'll get here as soon as she can. Oh, Helen, I wouldn't have invited her if I'd known. . . I thought she and dear Callum Priestley might—but I now see that he's far too good for her!'

'I've always liked her, that's the really funny part. . .'

'Are you *sure*, though? Nick is so. . .so upright.'

'Too upright, perhaps, to live a lie,' she managed miserably. 'He's realised he doesn't love me any more and—'

At Helen's frankly threatened tears, Gaye was suddenly brisk. 'Now, this is all nonsense. No, it *is*! You obviously need to have a good talk and sort things out, but I'm sure you'll find it's nothing.' She adopted a teasing tone. 'And I'm not having my domestic staff unable to do their duties because of love troubles, Mrs Darnell. You're about to let the soup boil, which won't do at all. Here's the tureen. . .'

She was right, of course, beyond the veneer of humour, and Helen was thankful to be able to bring the subject to a close. The two women worked steadily for ten minutes, chatting cheerfully about practicalities and bringing the soup, several quiches and casseroles, rice, stuffed vegetables, bread and salads out to the table.

'Serve yourselves,' Gaye announced, then returned to the kitchen to salvage the fruit salad after Claire and Sarah's well-meant but untidy efforts. She refused to let Helen join her. 'Because you can't go on brooding about it and dwelling on it. Socialise! The dress is lovely. Let Nick see a smile. Fight for your man! And, in any case, I'm sure you're wrong about it being serious.'

But her bright eyes didn't meet Helen's look full on as she said this last part, and Helen thought miserably, She doesn't want to believe I'm right, but she's afraid I might be.

She joined the queue for the buffet just behind Nick, who greeted her with a frown. Had she been deliberately avoiding him? 'Where did you get to?' he demanded, and it came out too much like an accusation.

'Helping Gaye.'

Innocent enough, he acknowledged, but there was a consciousness behind it. . . She and Gaye had been talking, of course, and he felt a hot spurt of anger. She needed to talk to *him*, not to a female friend—no matter how close. This was *their* marriage, *their* business, and she was leaving him out of whatever she was thinking. He felt horribly distanced from her; hated it; blamed both of them; felt the chafing burden of guilt. . .

And said only, 'So how was France?' Disguising as much of it all as he could, out of pride and hurt and goodness knew what else.

'France? Oh. . . I didn't ask,' she stammered.

'Didn't ask?'

Helen had grown immediately hot and knew she looked self-conscious. It was unnatural not to have asked Gaye about her summer, and betrayed very clearly the fact that she had been consumed with an agenda of her own. Suddenly it seemed wrong to have betrayed her fears about their marriage to a friend, albeit a close one, before she'd aired the issue with Nick himself, and he must have guessed that they had been having a heart-to-heart conversation because the frown that still pleated his high brow had become accusing. She felt ashamed and in the wrong.

'Gaye's a bit frazzled,' she explained hastily, with only

partial truthfulness. They couldn't get into a confrontation now. It would be unfair to their hosts. . .and all over the hospital by tomorrow morning. 'The girls weren't as much help as she'd hoped. We both forgot about France.'

'Hmm.' He turned from her, having reached the long table of food, and his rapidly heaped-up plate underlined Helen's own lack of appetite. A small bowl of soup and a bread roll would do, she decided.

Nick frowned at this as well, and she found herself thinking, Where's that dry, wicked smile I love, and that open laugh with his head thrown back? I never see those any more. . .

'I can't sit by and watch you eat barely enough to feed a mouse!' he exclaimed.

'Well, don't sit by, then!' she snapped back at him. 'Just sit somewhere else!'

He turned from her before she could see the result of her unnecessary sharpness in his face and it was at that moment that Megan entered, dressed in shimmering, beaded black. Since most people were still crowded around the buffet table the entrance to the large open-plan living and dining area was empty, and she made an attractive and dramatic figure standing there a little uncertainly, alone.

Having turned away from Helen and the other guests, Nick was at the edge of the crowded group now, and when Megan caught sight of him her eyes lit up. He moved towards her and she crossed the room to meet him halfway, her stride long and loping, just as Gaye pushed towards the table and announced in relief, 'More rice, everyone, so no need to ration yourselves.'

Helen pressed back against the wall with her meagre soup, and couldn't help watching the way Megan touched Nick on the arm as she greeted him. The blonde senior registrar was not able to conceal the sudden erotic heaviness of her lids and widening of her pupils, and the tip of her tongue had appeared, cat-like, between her full, darkly made-up lips.

Nick was murmuring something and, although he had his back to her, Helen caught a phrase, '. . .dressed like that. . .', which Megan responded to with a small laugh and a toss of her blonde head that was almost shy and oddly innocent. Her feelings were written all over her face.

Suddenly sick, Helen turned away from the sight of her husband and the woman who might already be his mistress and intercepted Gaye's shocked, instinctive glance, which was switching from Nick and Megan to herself. Earlier, in the kitchen, she had felt the older woman's gentle scepticism about the worst of her fears and it had gone a little way towards reassuring her.

Now she saw Gaye's horrified, helpless acknowledgement that those fears were well-grounded, and it was more than she could bear. Putting the untouched soup down on the nearest side-table, she fled upstairs to the softly lit landing and paced there on the carpet until Gaye joined her minutes later.

'It won't last, Helen. It can't last,' Gaye said fervently. 'He'd never be happy with someone like Megan. Don't just let it happen! Fight for him! Bring it out into the open!'

But Helen had reached a different conclusion. 'No,' she said stonily. 'That would only make it easier for him because I'm bound to get emotional and say things badly. He said tonight, just before we got here, that he wanted to talk. Well, let him talk, then! If he wants a divorce, then *he* can say the word. If he's having an affair with Megan, then *he* can tell me. I'm not going to bring it up. I'm not going to accuse him and play the harridan. If he wants a divorce, and this business of me not going to Boston is a preliminary to that, then let him tell me outright so we can at least put a veneer of civility on this.'

Helen felt her breathing coming in tight, short, painful

gasps, felt herself trembling, and knew that Gaye was watching her in mute concern, although her eyes were too tear blinded to see her friend clearly in the soft light.

'I must go down to the guests, Helen.' She was wringing her hands in an anguish of sympathy.

'Of course you must. I'm sorry to put you through this. It's my problem.'

'No, it isn't. It's Nick's,' Gaye returned crisply, 'and I never thought I'd ever be this angry with him!'

'Don't be!' It was terrible! She still loved him so much that she was defending him against an anger that Gaye was only feeling on her behalf. She groped for a rationale that would excuse him. 'Maybe it's my fault. I've been taking him for granted; forgetting to show my love; thinking too much about Jon and Jane at his expense because they were going away.'

'Helen, don't let him off the hook!'

'I must!' She was crying wildly now, and her scrap of handkerchief was useless. 'I'd far rather feel angry with myself than with him. Oh, that doesn't make sense! Oh, this is unbearable!'

'Use our bedroom, Helen. Take as long as you like. Use my make-up to redo your face. You can't have Nick or Megan seeing you like this.'

'Is that what it's come down to?' She managed a tight, bitter smile. 'A contest over make-up and looks? If it is, then Megan's going to win every time!'

'You *mustn't* let them see you like this!' Gaye repeated, then pushed Helen towards her open bedroom door and retreated swiftly down the carpeted stairs.

It took her half an hour to collect herself, cool her blotched and tear-stained face and apply some of Gaye's make-up to her red, over-scrubbed skin, and she found Nick just on his way up the stairs to look for her as she came down, still not sure that she was as composed as she wanted to be. He searched her face, that frown—which she now found so distancing—still in place.

'You OK? I didn't know where you'd got to.'

'I had a headache,' she lied convincingly. 'Gaye offered me a tablet and her bed. It's much better now.'

'Well, come and eat then before it's all cleared away. I saw your soup on the table. You hadn't touched it!'

He sounded impatient, as if she was being incomprehensibly foolish, and she didn't want to tell him that she had no appetite at all so she said flatly, 'I'll eat in the kitchen. Gaye's bound to need more help.'

She didn't meet his gaze, and could tell from his silhouette in her peripheral vision that he was growing more and more annoyed. He controlled it, however. 'Sure. Help Gaye. It's good that she's back now. I know you're missing Jon and Jane. We both are. . .'

And suddenly, so unexpectedly that she was almost crying again at once, his tone was sweet and tender and he was touching her, his hand brushing lightly against her jaw then down her back, to pull her tentatively closer. She felt the questing nudge of his nose and then his lips grazed hers, every nuance of their shape and taste familiar and utterly beloved. She lifted her face to respond, her own mouth quivering against him and tears springing like little diamonds onto her cheeks.

She felt one of them run down to disappear into the tight crevice between their joined mouths and he must have tasted the salt because he drew away and said, on a soft, questioning note, 'Helen?'

'Do you really love me, Nick?' She hated herself for asking the question with such tightly reined desperation, and it came out through clenched teeth.

He stiffened, and answered very quietly after a moment, 'Yes. I do. I always will.'

And the steadiness of it, the simplicity, didn't reassure her as she craved but only made her feel worse. He had sounded. . .*wooden*. . .as if his love was a duty—something he had undertaken to feel and would not renege on—and she thought that even if there was a divorce, even if there was a remarriage, yes, he would still love her in that honourable, dutiful way. She was, after all, the mother of his children. Nick was not a man in whom love turned frivolously into hatred or disdain. But was a bond of duty enough for either of them?

'I must help Gaye,' she managed, twisting free of his loose hold and heading for the kitchen without meeting his gaze again.

She knew, though, that he hadn't moved and was still watching her, and she wondered what he was feeling. Anger? Boredom? Pity? Or all of these, bound inextricably with the too-cool, too-steady flame of merely dutiful love?

Helen hid herself in the kitchen for the rest of the long, awful evening. Gaye genuinely needed her. The girls were tired and had relinquished their pound an hour for the lure of reading in bed before sleep. 'And I can't really blame them,' Gaye said. 'They had inter-school sport all morning, and were a wonderful help in the kitchen all afternoon before they started getting silly. Thanks for this, Helen. . .'

'I'd have been here even if you *hadn't* needed me,' she returned quietly, and nothing more was said as she began to tackle the dishes while Gaye took the array of desserts out to the table.

A little later she forced down some soup and a bit of chicken casserole with rice but couldn't summon any ability to eat the rich, sweet desserts at all, and went on with the dishes instead, scarcely aware of how late it was and that the other guests were starting to leave.

She reached the end of the huge pile of washing-up and went out to the living-room for the first time in two hours or more, intending to search for stray coffee-cups and cocktail glasses left behind in odd corners. The room was almost deserted now.

Nick was talking to Derek and Gaye, and Megan appeared to have been cornered by Callum Priestley, who was delivering an energetic monologue about a pressing professional issue. Helen caught some heavy medical terminology, then saw Megan's restless gaze leave Callum and dart to Nick, where it softened and lingered a little, before flicking back to Callum again.

Helen couldn't find any coffee-cups or cocktail glasses. Gaye must have done a thorough search herself before at last relaxing with her guests for the final half-hour of the evening. Callum had paused in his speech and his vigorous, ugly and oddly compelling face now looked uncertain as Megan's attention frankly left him.

'Helen,' she called.

'Yes, Megan?'

'I've hardly seen you.' She sounded cheerful, but looked guilty.

'I've been helping Gaye.'

'You look exhausted.' Why did Helen feel the comment was critical rather than compassionate?

Still, no point in denying the fact, as it became truer by the minute. 'I am rather,' she said.

'Why don't you go home to bed, then? You can take the car and I can easily give Nick a lift.'

'That's all right, Megan. I can hang on a few more minutes. I'm sure Nick's nearly ready to leave.'

They both looked across at him and Megan betrayed her scepticism with a raised eyebrow and a little smile. He and Derek were disgussing Paul Chambers's case and its wider implications.

'If we get a barrage of patients with infectious airborne diseases, exacerbated by HIV infection and needing full respiratory isolation, we just can't do it, Nick—you know we can't!' Derek was saying. 'Do you have any idea what I had to do to our budget just to get you that extra exhaust fan installed in his room at such short notice, not to mention the batch of particulate respirators, and now you want ultraviolet light as well?'

'Now, just a minute, Derek,' came Nick's strong, resonant voice. 'Don't make it sound as if this is just a whim on my part.'

Helen conceded victory to Megan. 'No, he's not ready yet, is he?' she said steadily. 'All right, then. I will take the car, and I won't interrupt him. Just let him know what's happening when he surfaces, will you?'

'Of course,' Megan answered in a bright, kind voice. 'Just go home and put your feet up.'

Those last words grated, with their connotation of aching legs and varicose veins, and yet Helen didn't think it was deliberately bitchy. Megan wasn't bitchy. She just wanted Nick to herself—perhaps she honestly thinks I don't mind—and she was as unthinkingly ambitious about this as she was about her career.

She wants to feel that I'm fifteen years older than she is instead of five because it assuages her conscience, Helen realised.

She managed to draw Gaye aside for a moment, thanked her for the evening and explained briefly what was happening. The older woman's eyes flashed with alarm and protest, but Helen responded wearily, 'Gaye, if it's happening, it's going to happen, and my stopping her from giving him a lift home isn't going to stand in the way.'

Still enveloped in her friend's shocked empathy, she let herself quietly out of the Wymans' house.

CHAPTER SIX

'WHAT on earth are you doing?' Nick reached Helen just as she opened the car door and, as she hadn't heard him coming, his voice startled her and her eyes were wide in the darkness as she looked up into his angry face.

'Didn't Megan explain?'

'I see you disappearing out the door with your bag in one hand and your car keys in the other, and Megan tells me I'm going home with her.'

'She offered. I thought you might be pleased. . .since you were pretty caught up in your debate with Derek.'

'Give me the chance to decide for myself, at least! Paul Chambers and his problems can wait. You and I were going to talk and the whole evening went by with you in the kitchen like a navvy, or up on Derek and Gaye's bed.'

'Oh. Sorry I had a headache,' she snapped. 'Anyway, are you suggesting this "talk" should have taken place in the midst of a party?'

'Of course not! Don't be ridiculous! But we could have left at least an hour and a half ago without being rude. Now, it's nearly a quarter to one.'

'All right,' she responded stiffly, flinching at his anger—which seemed to resonate more deeply tonight, as if it had an underlying cause that was more significant than the petty words themselves. 'Since we're tired, let's postpone this to a more convenient time.'

'No! I want to know what this is all about, Helen. What's got into you?'

'Into *me*?' She shook her head in disbelief and the stubbornness she had felt earlier surged back again, stronger than ever. She *would not* be the one to mention divorce, or to say Megan's name. He was the one who didn't want her to go to Boston. He was the one creating this. . .wasn't he?

'You're saying this is. . .*my* fault?' Outwardly he seemed less angry now, more thoughtful.

'Well, isn't it?' she shot back, then added remorsefully. 'No! No! I can't say that, can I? In a marriage like ours that can never be true. It's my fault too. But the difference is that you don't seem to care.'

'Not care? Of course I care! Would we be talking like this if I didn't care?'

'So it's not. . .too late, then?' she whispered. They still hadn't touched but now he reached out and held her and she felt the tension and wariness in him, which, instinctively, she tried to soothe away.

Pillowing her head against the bulwark of his chest and feeling his arms warm around her, she heard the resonance of his voice against her ear, speaking in that same careful, wooden way in which he had said that, yes, he would always love her. 'I hope it's not too late, Helen. I'm prepared to try as hard as I can, and I'm sure we can put this period behind us.'

She tried to meet him halfway, wishing that the words would come more easily for both of them. 'And perhaps if. . .if things are going well, we could. . .reconsider the Boston idea.'

'You're asking me not to go?' He released her a little, and stared down.

'No, I mean, perhaps I could come with you after all.' Her heart was pounding as she made the suggestion. If he said no to this, then their talk, stiff and clumsy as it was, had meant nothing.

There was a long pause before he spoke, and he seemed to be searching very carefully for the right words. Behind them Callum Priestley came out to his car and drove away, with an economical salute in their direction.

'I'd like that, Helen,' Nick said finally. Another pause.

He seemed terribly at sea, and was holding her as if she might break. . .or fly away like a captured bird. 'Don't let's make. . .rash promises, though. You may find, after all, that you want it as a way out. *Not* going, I mean. Let's be honest. What we said about the twins and your job was just papering it over, wasn't it?'

'Yes.' Her reply was very low. So this was honesty, was it? This careful, wooden stuff.

'The real reason. . .makes sense, perhaps. That—'

And suddenly she was too impatient to wait for his measured words. 'That a year apart would make an easy preliminary to divorce?' she cut in sharply. There! After all her resolve, she had still been the first one to mention the word that lately had been drumming with such an ugly rhythm in her head.

She heard his hissing intake of breath. They were still holding each other, clutching each other stiffly now, and it held no comfort. All it did was help her read more clearly the signals coming from his familiar body. This tightness in every muscle, this iron control in him. Guilt? An attempt to conceal relief?

'God, that's a word I never thought we'd be saying to each other!' His laugh was harsh.

'No, neither did I, but, as Megan pointed out, we're already in a statistical minority, marrying so young and still together.' There, again! Megan's name, when she had been so determined not to say it.

He said in an odd tone, 'You've talked about this to Megan?'

She managed a laugh. 'It was more that *she* talked about it to me.'

'I see. . . Helen, Megan is more naïve and gauche than she might seem, at times. Just because—'

And then, suddenly, Megan herself was there, coming towards them—her walk rapid and her arms angular and awkward as she balanced on her high heels in the gravel of the drive. 'Nick, Helen, I didn't think you'd left yet. . .'

Helen instantly wondered, Why? Has she been watching from the window, hoping it would escalate into a big fight?

'What is it, Megan?' Nick asked sharply.

'Derek. He's been taken ill, and I thought you should be the one to—'

'Ill?'

'Yes, very suddenly. And I'm afraid my dress caught the brunt. . .' She trailed off, brushing at her beautiful dress with the towel that was pressed to it, and Helen glimpsed the unsightly stains.

'We'll come straight in, Megan,' she said to the younger woman, not unkindly. 'You go home and change if you want to.'

The senior registrar explained anxiously, 'I'm on call, you see. Even a white coat wouldn't cover this.'

'Get it dry-cleaned straight away, or it'll be ruined.' Although Helen privately considered the dress rather overdone with its elaborate encrusting of beads and sequins.

Nick was already on his way inside and she hurried after him, with Megan beside her. 'I must make sure Nick doesn't need me before I go,' the latter said breathily.

It became a battle between the gravel and their heels and Helen, with her more modest ones, won it to enter the Wymans' house again shortly after her husband. She met Gaye, who alternated between laughing and wringing her hands.

'This is ridiculous! It must be food-poisoning, I'm sure, but Derek is panicking. He's been out of day-to-day medicine himself for so many years, he always thinks the worst of the slightest symptoms.'

'Where is he?' Nick wanted to know.

'In the bathroom. . .*again*! It came on so suddenly. Megan started to examine him, and. . . Well, you saw what happened to the poor girl! You see, he's sure it's a dissecting aneurysm or an infarction, or goodness knows what rare and fatal syndrome. But then he had to dash for the loo, and Megan couldn't—'

'I'm sorry,' Megan apologised in the background. 'My dress, you see. Nick, the symptoms add up for food poisoning but, as Derek rightly fears, there are some more serious emergencies which can present in a similar—'

'I'll look at him, Megan.' His tone was rather abrupt, then, 'Helen, darling, ring the hospital and tell Casualty we're coming in. Then do some detective work with Gaye. It's alarming that no one else is affected. We all ate the same things. And if it's *not* food poisoning. . .'

Derek emerged from the guest bathroom beneath the stairs at that moment, white-faced and clammy-skinned. While Helen waited on the phone, Nick had him lie on the couch and he did so reluctantly, still in the grip of abdominal pain and warning, through gritted teeth, that another visit to the bathroom was imminent.

'Tender here?'

'No. . .'

'Here?'

'No. It was just so damned sudden. . . Excuse me, Nick, I've got to go.' And he lunged down the hall again.

'They're quiet at the moment,' Helen reported, having successfully contacted Casualty.

'No localised tenderness, which is a good sign, but there's still the worrying factor that no one else is suffering.'

'Yes,' Helen said. 'I've been thinking about everything we served. Those quiches, of course, would be a prime suspect.'

'Yes, but they got polished off down to the last crumb. Everyone ate them,' Gaye protested. 'I had a slice of the asparagus one and the crab meat.'

'And I had the Florentine and the plain cheese,' Nick said. 'And they were delicious, Gaye, by the way.'

'Oh, absolutely!' Megan came in, still hovering awkwardly in her soiled dress.

She looked tired and uncomfortable and, albeit unwillingly, Helen felt sorry for her. Megan's eyes were glued to Nick, but he was ignoring her totally. Was he angry at her for launching that betraying discussion of divorce rates in early marriages? For some reason Helen suddenly felt better about the whole thing than she had done for nearly three weeks.

In this medical crisis, which could yet turn out to be a major one, Nick's every instinct was to turn to her, not to Megan, although the latter was a doctor. That had to mean something, surely, if only that their marriage still had a chance of being saved. Though concerned about Derek, Helen still couldn't help feeling that a dull weight had been partially lifted from her shoulders.

'No, it can't be the quiche,' Nick was saying.

'The stuffed courgettes!' It came to Helen quite suddenly as she remembered her black hours in the kitchen over the clearing up.

Derek had come in halfway through the process to graze on leftovers, having been too busy replenishing his guests' drinks earlier to eat a proper meal. He had taken one of the courgette halves, still lukewarm and stuffed with an appetising mixture of lamb, rice and herbs and topped with tomato and melted cheese, and gulped a huge mouthful.

'Aagh! Bitter!' he had exclaimed.

'Really?' Helen had been surprised. She'd seen other people eating them with no complaint.

'I'll try another.' He had thrown the first one away and then bolted two more, pronouncing them perfectly all right, before returning to his guests.

'But the filling in those was fairly harmless, wasn't it?' Gaye protested.

'Not the filling, the courgette itself,' Helen said. 'Isn't it true that something like one in ten thousand courgettes contains a natural toxin? I read it. Nick, you'd know.

Derek said one of them was very bitter and he didn't finish it.'

'Really? That's it, then!' Nick's expression cleared and only then did Helen realise that he must have been seriously concerned, both because of the sudden onset of the symptoms and the fact that Derek was alone in suffering. 'He should still go to Casualty. We'll take him, Helen, as soon as he's over this attack. He'll need intravenous fluids, and I still want to suggest some tests. Gaye. . .?'

'I'd like to come, but I can't leave the girls alone in the house at this hour of the night.' She flicked a tiny glance in Megan's direction, clearly hoping for an offer to stay with them, but Megan didn't see it and didn't make the suggestion on her own, and then Helen remembered that she was on call. Megan was blinking and yawning behind her fist, though trying desperately not to show it.

'Go home, Megan,' Nick ordered.

'No, no, really. . .'

'*Go home*! I'm not being polite. You're on call, and you must change.'

She looked chastened at once, and her gaze beseeched his forgiveness, giving her face a youthful, suppliant quality. Helen saw Nick reach out to pat her arm, and Megan gave a tremulous smile. What an odd creature she was! Such a mixture of sophistication and uncertainty.

'Of course you're right, Nick,' she breathed fervently, as if he'd just discovered penicillin, and Helen saw a fleeting frown cross Nick's face—as if he was annoyed at the woman's betrayal of her feelings for him. She gritted her teeth and tried to ignore the expression, determined not to dwell on its significance. Maybe he'd just let himself flirt with her in Boston and was now regretting it. She could forgive that, couldn't she?

'Let's get to the hospital now, before the next wave

of it comes,' Derek said, emerging weakly from the bath-room once again.

A minute later they were off, and Nick explained about their theory of the poisonous courgette, which visibly reassured the medical administrator.

'It did taste vile,' Derek growled. 'I should have spat it out, but it took me by surprise. Sorry to be putting you through this at this hour. Perhaps it isn't even necessary.'

'It is,' Nick said. 'I don't have to tell you. You're a doctor. At the very least you're going to need fluids.'

'Yes, and the loo again any minute,' poor Derek groaned.

They reached Casualty just in time and, as Derek was being settled into a cubicle, Nick quietly conferred with the registrar on call and they decided on a couple of tests just to make sure. Helen rang Gaye to say that they had arrived safely, and that Derek would stay in Casualty for what remained of the night.

It was after two o'clock by the time she and Nick finally reached home, and they both fell into bed after making their night preparations in a silence that spoke of weariness far more than distance. *If he touches me, I'll be able to believe that it's going to be all right*, was Helen's last coherent thought, and he did touch her, wrapping his arm around her from behind, just as she slipped into sleep so that she drifted away on a feeling of happiness and hope.

It was nine-thirty before Helen stirred the next morning to find Nick propped up on one elbow, watching her quizzically, with his dark grey eyes containing that twinkling hint of humour that she loved so well.

'What are you doing?' she said sleepily. 'Not called out?'

'No, I'm off until tomorrow, remember?'

'Then. . .?'

'Just trying to decide how we should celebrate.'

'Celebrate?'

'Our first morning to lie in bed together, alone in the house, in—what—eighteen years?'

'Our first?'

'Yes, when you think about it. Last weekend I had too much work, the weekend before I was in Boston and the weekend before that we were delivering Jonathon and Jane to London. Oh, I suppose there have been other times in recent years when they've been away, but somehow. . .'

'Oh. . . Yes. . . It's luxurious, isn't it, but somehow it makes me feel sad, too. It's quite probable that they'll never really be back here to live again.'

'What a mother you are!'

'I know.' She made a face. 'I'm—I'm finding it quite hard, Nick.'

'I know, my pearl of a thousand pearls.' His voice was tender and light at the same time.

'Hen of a thousand hens, you mean, clucking like this! Just tell me they're not going to do anything really silly in London on their own!' Apart from that engagement, which was such a sore and contentious point that she dismissed it firmly from her mind at once.

'Well, when I rang them from Boston,' Nick was saying earnestly, 'Jane did say that she'd dyed her hair green. Did I mention that? Oh, and Jonathon has decided to go for the world speed record in blood-pudding consumption. He's training twice a day, apparently. We should be very proud of his commitment, I think. So far he's managed to down fourteen of them in—'

A pillow, stuffed unceremoniously into Nick's face, cut off the flow. 'Seriously, though,' she said when she released him at last. 'This *is* nice. What shall we do?'

'Breakfast in bed for starters?'

'At the very least!'

This was more like it! They made it together in the kitchen—eggs and bacon, sausages and tomatoes, toast and coffee and fresh-squeezed juice. Helen was bundled into a silk kimono and Nick looked tall and ludicrously masculine in a navy blue nightshirt of soft cotton that Jane had given him for Christmas, informing him kindly that pyjamas were quite *passé*. Then they giggled in bed like children having a midnight feast, fought over sections of the Sunday paper and spilled toast crumbs.

'Mmm,' he growled throatily when his coffee was finished, 'I could go to sleep again.'

'Could you?'

'Or. . .?' He didn't need to finish. They smiled at each other in silence for several long seconds, then Helen realised to her amazement that she was blushing and could no longer meet his liquid grey gaze.

Reaching out for her, he pulled off the silk kimono lazily, then his hands nudged and whispered against the fine lawn nightdress beneath until she took pity on him and lifted it over her head to sit there, naked, in a tangle of floral sheets while he pulled impatiently at his own garment and then flung it aside. She lunged at him with a fluid movement and they fell back onto the pillows together to begin the familiar journey of discovery that was their love-making.

With the doubts that still nagged at the edge of her mind, Helen's surrender to this most physical part of their marriage was total. Her kisses pulled at his mouth until he nibbled her hungrily in return, and her name on his lips was repeated with surprise and then pleasure and then throaty ardour at the feline aggression she was showing. She couldn't seem to find enough of him to fill her hands and her palms slid over his body feverishly, glorying in the textured patterns of silken skin and rough hair.

She tasted him, from the faint coffee flavour of his mouth to the muskiness of the hair on his chest, trailing lower and lower. His groans told her how much he relished her abandoned exploration, the touches and caresses she made which were like statements of possession. This wonderful, strong, familiar body belonged to her—*had* to belong to her—just as her own satiny skin and the female fullness of her breasts belonged utterly to him.

When at last they joined together the way he filled her, weighed upon her and drank her kiss, had her on the edge of tears and trembling until she was swept away beyond any thought at all into a landscape of pure physical and emotional release. Afterwards, they lay quietly as they always did and, sensing the heavy rhythm of his breathing, she did not fight her own drowsiness so that they both slept again, and it was well after eleven before his creaky voice echoed her own thought.

'Lucky we didn't have to get to Liz and Pete's in time for lunch. . .'

'We do have to get there at some point, though. . .'

'I know, and it's an hour and a half's drive. What do you fancy? A shower. . .together. . .and then a stop along the way for a snack?'

'Not hungry at all, yet. Just some fruit, maybe, because Liz and Pete are bound to heap us with tea and cake and sandwiches.'

Later, after a silly, sexy soap fight in the shower which almost led to another session in bed, Helen hardly dared to talk in the car as they drove in case she said something that would spoil this magical restoration of closeness and harmony. Nick was silent, too, but that tell-tale tightening of shoulders and hardness of eyes was gone. She couldn't help watching him secretly as he drove—his strong hands on the wheel, his face focused yet relaxed and his grey eyes fixed steadily on the road ahead.

Her heart turned over, and her breath caught tightly in her chest. Is he really still mine? How on earth would I bear it if he wasn't? I couldn't, could I? Life wouldn't be worth living any more. . . She shook off the thought.

In the air between them today there was no hint of such a thing.

It was a gorgeous day, mild and sunny, with only soft clouds buffing the skyline to the south. The fields were still green and lush and dotted with black-faced sheep, and the old converted mill where the Holloways lived dreamed and sunned itself above the race of the river beside it. Carrot-topped Pete met them in the yard and brought them straight around to the wooden deck he had made in the sheltered sun-trap between the 'L' of the mill's stone walls.

'Liz is lying down. She's really not supposed to get up much these days.'

'She's due very soon, isn't she?' Helen asked.

'Two weeks. That's already *overdue* when it comes to twins, apparently.'

'Yes, Jon and Jane didn't last the full distance.' In fact, they'd had to have a week in the special care nursery before coming home, but it wouldn't be kind to mention that today. 'How is she feeling?'

'I'm fine.' Liz had heard their approach and was on her feet, brushing aside her husband's protests. 'Honestly, it doesn't matter now. How are Jon and Jane in the big city?'

'Well, Jane's engaged, bless her!' Nick said.

'No, not "bless her"!' Helen blurted, not able to restrain herself on the subject this time. 'It's terrible, and I can't think why you keep announcing it as if it was good news!'

But once again Nick only tut-tutted her feelings away, then stared silently into his lap. She was angry with him, felt he was patronising her, and had to make an effort to push her sudden resentment aside for Liz's and Pete's sakes. The Holloways, understandably, hadn't known how to respond. Congratulations? Commiserations? It was embarrassing, and completely Nick's fault, Helen felt.

Fortunately, Liz was already pouring out tea, her loose, nut-brown hair falling forward to hide her face. She uncovered plates of cake and scones and sandwiches then lay back on her outdoor lounger, looking heavy and slow and dreamy and ripely ready to deliver.

Helen took a scone and sipped her tea, still searching for something safe to say, then suddenly realised, 'Liz, you haven't got a cup!'

And her friend of more than twenty years said calmly and with a note of tentative apology, 'I shouldn't, I don't think. I've been in labour for nearly two hours.'

The quiet statement electrified the other three, and immediately any awkwardness over the issue of Jane's doomed engagement was forgotten. Nick sprang to his feet as if he'd been shot. He spilled his tea onto the ground and clutched at his chest with splayed fingers as if expecting to find a stethoscope there, with which to listen to the baby at once. Pete had turned pale and held a sandwich halfway to his mouth in a frozen, appalled gesture, his mouth sagging idiotically. Helen let her tea-cup fall back into its saucer with a clatter.

Liz herself merely smiled. 'Please don't panic. I'm an "elderly primip", remember? Prime candidate for a long labour. We're hours away from anything happening. The contractions are very mild and only just getting up to once every twenty minutes.'

'My God, so *that's* why you kept asking me the time? I thought you were wondering when Helen and Nick were going to get here!' her husband spluttered. 'Why didn't you tell me?'

'Because I wanted to see Helen and Nick, and I knew if I told you you'd want to cancel them,' Liz pointed out reasonably.

'Of course I would have!'

'See! There you are, then! Everything feels fine, and I can still feel nice vigorous movements from the babies. Helen's a nurse. Nick's a doctor. . .'

But Helen laughed and Nick grinned sheepishly, his grey gaze flicking to meet hers in a moment of shared understanding before he addressed Liz. 'You wouldn't know it, would you? I confess I panicked at your announcement, and every rusty vestige of my obstetric skills left my head at once!'

'Oh, rubbish! I'd trust you to deliver me in the middle of a bridge in a thunderstorm, Nick!'

'Thank you,' he responded humbly.

'Do phone your doctor, Liz,' Helen urged. 'He might want you to come in.'

'Nonsense! I'll phone him soonishly, but he's already told me not to come in until the contractions are five minutes apart—unless anything unexpected is happening, and so far it *isn't*. It's all just like we learned in our NCT classes. *Please* don't go into a tizzy, all of you.'

'Liz, ah, could I get my trusty little stethoscope, though?' Nick pleaded, fidgeting. 'It's in my bag in the car. I'm being very doctorish, I know, and I won't if you don't want me to, but if we're going to sit here and relax and chat I'd just like to *know* that those baby heartbeats sound the way they should.'

'Take pity on him, Lizzie,' her husband groaned, 'because I'd like to know it too.'

'Oh, go ahead, you technological males,' Liz laughed. 'I can tell they're perfectly all right, but if you need whizz-bang metal gadgetry in your hands for reassurance. . .'

Nick glowered comically, unswayed in his determination, and was back from the car in half a minute, brandishing the beloved instrument with evident satisfaction. In the end they all took a turn to listen, and it was a surprisingly emotional time. First Helen watched Nick, his dark head bending forward and his fingertips questing very lightly and tenderly over Liz's distended abdomen, and a broad and somehow very youthful smile lit up his face when he found the two fast-paced heartbeats. It brought back memories. . .

Then it was Pete's turn and he muttered creakily at the sounds, 'Can't believe it. . . Can't wait. . . Hell, I hope it's all OK.' He squeezed Liz's hand as she listened, her own smile full of a magical anticipation.

Lastly came Helen. It must be years since she'd heard those rapid beats—during the obstetrics component of her general training and before that with her own twins, of course. Heavens, over eighteen years ago and yet schoolfriend Liz, at almost exactly Helen's own age, was only just starting out on the long journey of motherhood. . .

I want to have another baby.

The knowledge, profound and emotional, ambushed her out of nowhere and had her weak-kneed at once, her mind buzzing. Did she really? Could she go through it all again? She thought of the years of fatigue, the feeling of being splintered into three different roles—wife, mother, and nurse—with none of them leaving any time to lavish on her own needs.

Was that really what she wanted? No! And yet she *did* want a baby. Differently, this time. She wanted to be able to give up work. They could afford that now. She wanted some help, too. Someone to come in a couple of times a week so that having a baby didn't have to mean an untidy house and exhaustion and poorly planned meals. There was so much of Jon's and Jane's childhood that she hadn't been able to enjoy because there had been too much else to do and to think of.

This time, she wanted to relish every second of it. She saw herself in some wonderful, quirky house like this one, and—

That was when she knew that it was all just a fantasy. They didn't live in a wonderful, quirky house; they lived in a very practical brick bungalow, and Nick wouldn't want another baby. Of course he wouldn't! She wouldn't even dare to ask.

He had put his stethoscope away now and received the fresh cup of tea that Pete had poured for him to replace the one he had spilled. Liz was having a contraction. She winced and shifted uncomfortably. 'Hmm, that one hurt a bit. What's the time, Pete?'

'Twenty-six minutes past three. Here, you wear the watch, darling.'

'Seventeen minutes. OK.' She sat back again.

'Is there anything I can get to make you more comfortable, Liz?' Helen asked quickly.

'Actually, my sandals. They're inside by the couch. I think I'd like to walk around a bit—along the path by the river. They say that's supposed to speed things up. And would you walk with me?'

'As long as you promise not to deliver out in the open. My midwifery skills aren't up to scratch any more.'

It was a very pleasant time. They just walked slowly up and down the path along the river-bank, with Helen helping Liz to breathe through the contractions which had begun to come with increasing frequency and strength. They didn't talk much. Names for the babies. Pete's gallantly concealed nerves about the whole thing. Helen felt a strong urge to confess the disturbingly maternal yearning she had just discovered in herself, but resisted. Liz would only encourage her, and really it was impossible. Just impossible.

Then . . . 'Oh!' Liz looked down in surprise as her print maternity dress and bare legs were suddenly soaked with a flood of clear liquid. 'That's my waters.'

A strong contraction came almost immediately—just ten minutes since the previous one. It was a quarter to five already. 'Perhaps it's time to think about going in,' Helen suggested.

Liz nodded. 'The hospital's twenty minutes away.'

The men were talking seriously when they got back.

Helen could hear it in their voices before she got close enough to make out the words. Pete turned to her as she approached and said, 'Nick's been telling me about Boston.' But that was a word Helen was beginning to hate. It must have showed in her face.

'You're not looking forward to it?' Pete wanted to know, surprised.

Nick came in steadily, 'It's not definitely decided yet whether Helen is to go.'

'Not *go*?' This was Liz, at Helen's side.

'It might be best if she stays behind,' Nick explained.

He felt wooden and not very sincere, and wondered painfully if Helen wouldn't contradict him—tell these old friends what she really thought about it all underneath. Was he a coward, or would it be best after all if they just did drift apart? After this morning...their laughter...his hands on her skin and cupping her lovely breasts, soap-covered, in the shower, he rebelled completely.

Then he remembered what Megan had said over dinner in Boston that night which was so strongly engraved on his memory. Leaning earnestly towards him, her eyes shining like her glamorous dress in the glow of the restaurant lighting. He'd heard again her opinions—and Helen's, apparently, as he had always secretly feared—about what a young marriage did to limit a woman's options for fulfillment. Megan herself had deliberately waited until her thirties, it seemed, before thinking about settling down. Because of him, Helen hadn't allowed herself that luxury...

He took a careful breath then explained mechanically to Pete, hiding what he felt, 'You see, there's the question of leaving the twins, and the house. Not to mention Helen's job...'

'And the cat,' Helen couldn't help adding tersely, to complete a litany that was beginning to grate considerably.

She noticed that Nick had carefully managed to make it sound like a joint idea, something they were weighing the pros and cons of together, instead of something that had come from him out of the blue and been discussed only in the most stilted phrases.

'But, Helen, we could take the cat, for goodness' sake!' Liz said, and Helen found herself explaining that dear old Pushcart wouldn't react well to a move, as if the sedate tabby really was involved in the issue.

Nick moved irritably. 'It's idiotic to be discussing this now,' he said, his grey eyes restless and brooding and hard. 'Liz, have you phoned your doctor?' He'd seen the spreading wetness on her print dress.

'No, I'm on my way in to do it now.'

'What?' Pete said, then saw the dress as well. 'Oh. . .' He turned pale. 'Is everything in your hospital bag, Liz? I'll put it in the car. And I must take these dishes in. God, we're going to be up all night, I suppose. Where are my keys?'

Nick nudged him gently inside in the wake of Liz who, remaining calm, had gone to the phone, then he and Helen cleared up the afternoon tea things. They finished just as Liz and Pete were ready to leave.

'Sorry not to be better hosts,' Pete said, still distracted.

Liz was fretting now, too, in the wake of a contraction that had brought real pain. 'I forgot my brush! Did I? No, I think it's in. Oh, doesn't matter! I want to get going. Oh, dear, Helen, how did you ever get through this?'

Car doors slammed, Liz and Pete drove away and Nick and Helen followed in their wake, silent until the car ahead of them turned off in a different direction to head to the hospital. Not Camberton Hospital, of course. That was over an hour away along the route that Helen and Nick now took.

'Strange to think that Liz and Pete are just starting out, and we've pretty much finished,' he said slowly as the other car disappeared down the hill.

'Yes,' Helen managed, mourning the unmistakable death of her fantasy about a baby. Well, had it been at all realistic? No. . .

The closeness between the two of them that had come after the Wymans' party last night seemed to have gone again; had perhaps been just an illusion created by sharing a pleasant day off, and by their sensual appetites for each other in bed

So how could she even be thinking about a baby when she didn't know for certain that she still had a marriage?

CHAPTER SEVEN

'I HAVE to apologise for that suggestion I made to you three weeks ago about Paul Chambers,' Stella Harris said to Helen rather pleadingly, turning to her at the conclusion of a brief midday meeting of community nursing staff and general practitioners at the South Camberton Health Centre. Helen had come straight here from her Monday morning single mothers' group. 'I had no idea then, of course, that he had multi-drug-resistant TB. Good heavens, he looked so healthy and strong. To think if he'd delayed going to the doctor and you'd taken my advice!'

'I never really had any intention of taking it, Stella,' Helen answered gently, then she added, 'Although, in fact, I like Paul Chambers. He's a very interesting man.'

It was true that he was interesting. Not quite true that she liked him. She was too wary of him for that. But she recognised his arrogant, animal power and, yes, his sexual allure, and wondered whether she'd have to start noting those things about men again somewhere down the line. If Nick went to Boston alone and if that separation then grew into a permanent one, followed by a divorce. . .

My God, what would it be like to be 'out there' again? Being single in the 1990s at thirty-seven was a far different thing from being single in the 1970s at fifteen. That long ago she hadn't thought of herself as 'single'.

She'd married Nick because they just felt so overwhelmingly right together, not because she'd had any particular ambition to marry and settle down young. The opposite, really. She had intended to travel, experience life in another part of the world. It would be ironic,

wouldn't it, if their marriage foundered just when she
and Nick might have been able to travel and live abroad
together?

Paul Chambers was a travelling man, and Karen
Graham certainly didn't seem to feel that his disease
made him less attractive. Perhaps I should make a play
for him, Helen thought. But the idea nauseated her at
once, and she went shaky again at the thought of being
without Nick.

Stella Harris was still hovering nearby. 'You and Dr
Snaith asked at the meeting if anyone else was interested
in becoming involved in the emphysema support
group. . .'

'Yes. You are? Lovely!' Helen concealed her surprise.
Until this point Stella had kept strictly to her prescribed
duties in the community, and showed little interest or
initiative beyond what was required on paper.

Now, she said, 'Yes. I—I'm looking for more to do.
I've been brooding too much and that helps no one, least
of all myself. The idea of the group caught my attention.
My father was a heavy smoker and died of lung cancer
in the end. He always said that he found the emphysema
harder to bear.

'I've realised that if I don't do something to help other
people—take my mind off my own problems—I'm never
going to get over my anger at Raymond. It's already
eaten away at far too much of what I've always valued
in myself. Is that. . .? Perhaps that's a bad reason for
wanting to volunteer,' she finished. 'It's a selfish one.

'Stella, no, of course it isn't a bad reason!' Helen
exclaimed. 'My goodness, if we had to wait for a bolt
of pure selflessness to hit us from the blue before we
did anything, charity would have died out long ago. My
interest isn't exactly unprejudiced, either. Nick sees so
many emphysema patients. If I can do something to take
the onus off him, in helping these people and supporting

their efforts to stop smoking, then I'll have a happier husband at home.'

'Can't quarrel with that reasoning,' Stella laughed, the bitterness falling from her face for a moment.

She's on the mend, Helen realised. At last! It takes a long time...

Stella left the health centre to do some errands and Helen was about to take out the packet of sandwiches she had brought from home when the phone rang on her desk, put through from the main switch in Reception out the front. It was Pete Holloway, sounding exhausted and exuberant and close to tears all at once. 'Safely delivered. An hour ago. Both boys. With my red hair! Healthy as anything, though Stephen's a little smaller than Chris. Liz did brilliantly! They're so...*alive*! I can't believe it!'

'Pete, that's wonderful!'

They talked for five minutes—incoherent and exultant on Pete's side, warm and secretly just a little wistful on Helen's. Nick must have sounded like this eighteen years ago on the phone to parents and cousins and friends. Putting down the phone, Helen had to pick it up again almost immediately when it rang once more, and this time she heard the far less welcome voice of Megan Stone.

Her tone was brittle and high. 'I'll be over your way in about five minutes, and I wondered if I could drop in for a chat. Is—is there somewhere we could go?'

'There's a café in the shops just down the road,' Helen said reluctantly. Her spine crawled with suspicion at this cheery overture. Why would Megan be 'over this way'?

'So I'll meet you at the front of your building, shall I?' Her voice was still high and brittle. 'And we can go on from there.'

'All right. I'll see you in a few minutes.'

Helen put down the phone and began to gobble her sandwiches. She was hungry and, short of eating in the car this afternoon on her way to her first home visit, this was the only chance she would get. Eating too fast didn't improve her mood, and she was as tense and brittle in manner as Megan appeared to be when the latter climbed out of her sleek red car just three minutes later than the time she had nominated. She wore a beautifully cut but rather severe navy suit which emphasised the fair sheen of her blonde hair and, as always, she stood several inches taller than Helen in her high-heeled shoes.

They walked to the nearby line of shops, parroting platitudes about the weather, which had turned colder, and Helen realised, She's incredibly nervous, although she thinks she's hiding it.

Once seated, they both ordered hot drinks immediately. Tea for Helen and black coffee for Megan, then the latter said, as soon as the waitress was out of earshot, 'Nick says you're thinking of going to Boston after all.'

'Yes. I am.' Helen didn't tell her that, actually, she'd never thought of *not* going. That had all been Nick's idea.

'Don't.'

'*What*?'

'I—I think it might be better if you don't go.'

Helen was speechless.

'Don't you see how unfair it is?' Megan went on in a desperate tone. Helen saw that her hands were shaking and her mouth looked pale and miserable. 'Your staying behind was the perfect solution. Civilised, decent and honourable. You must know what an honourable man Nick is! If you have any feeling left for him at all, can't you make this a little easier on him?'

'I'm not sure that I quite follow you, Megan,' Helen said tightly.

'Oh, don't you? Yes, you do!' the younger woman insisted distractedly, seizing the coffee that had just arrived and chafing the hot sides of the cup with tightly held fingers.

'First of all, are you saying that you and my husband are sleeping together?' Deliberately, she put it in the harshest terms she could think of, and had the grim satisfaction of seeing Megan's gaze falter and fall.

'No, not yet,' she said, after a tiny pause. 'Of course we're not! Nick's too decent for that, as you must know. He wouldn't let himself be physically unfaithful until he was satisfied that his marriage was really over.'

'And what makes you so sure that it is?' Helen's clipped tones betrayed nothing of her inner agony.

'Oh, it—it must be! When you married so young. My parents did, and they're miserable. It's sickening!' Megan shook this subject off as a digression, then seemed to land on surer ground. 'I've thought about it. I've discussed it with Nick. What can possibly be holding you together? The children and society's conventions, that's all. And now the children have left.'

Helen felt a sudden, twisting pang at Megan's offhand phrase, as if Jon and Jane were totally gone from her life and she would never see them again. But that was quite ridiculous, and shouldn't unsettle her!

'The two of you have got nothing in common, Helen, as you must see yourself,' Megan continued. 'Your understanding of his work is. . .well, not exactly on a par. You're wrapped up in your children and your job at his expense. You're far from being his intellectual equal.' She stopped and back-pedalled a little, looking ashamed.

'No, sorry, that's not true, I expect. And it's not your fault. You never had the chance to become anything more than a nurse, marrying and becoming a mother so young. Please don't think that I hate you or wish you ill in any way.' She was actually pleading now, desperately sincere.

'I'm simply asking you to be realistic about this, and not go to Boston. Nick and I are in love, and if you would only step aside with grace—and you *are* a very graceful and wonderful woman, Helen, I've always thought so—then Nick will have a chance at the deeper happiness he deserves. We were both so incredibly alive during that week in Boston. We went walking in the old

part of the city, and up to Beacon Hill. . . We had dinner
together twice. . . If you could have seen him, you—'

'You and Nick—' Helen interjected desperately
through numb lips, but Megan interrupted in her turn,
leaning eagerly forward.

'I've spoken so frankly to you because I respect you,
Helen, and I hope you know that. I think we can all come
out of this with dignity if we tackle it in the right way.
Please don't think that I want you to be hurt!'

It would have been easier for her if Megan *had* wanted
that, Helen thought. She could have dismissed someone
who was clearly a cold-blooded, calculating siren.
Megan, with her earnest appeals to Helen's decency and
her obvious expectation that this could and should be easy
for all three of them, demanded to be taken seriously.

She tried to speak once again, hearing the unsteadiness
in her own voice. 'It seems that. . .you and Nick have
discussed all this. Does he know you're here with
me now?'

'No, he doesn't,' Megan said, her confidence faltering
for a moment. Then she regrouped. 'If you really knew
him, you'd know he's not the sort of person to talk and
connive about these things. He's going to need time and
distance before he feels fully free to establish a relationship, and that's what I'm asking you to give us. That's
all I'm asking you to give us at this stage.'

'I—'

'You don't really want to force Nick into limping
along with you for another twenty years, do you?' Megan
demanded quietly. 'You wouldn't want that for yourself, either.'

'No, of course I don't, if ''limping'' is what we're
doing,' Helen said, surprised at the calm and control in
her voice. A huge part of her felt that this scene couldn't
really be happening at all. It was like a film and she was
watching herself, watching the small section of herself

that was able, somehow, to play the required part in this civilised duel.

'No, well, as I said, that's the sort of thing I respect in you, Helen.' Megan had already risen from the table, her coffee still pooling darkly halfway to the top of the cup. Helen hadn't even got as far as pouring her own tea. 'And I promise you, if you still care about this, that I'll do everything I can to make him happy.' She dropped some notes on the table for the bill. 'I—I have to get back to the hospital now. I'm late already.'

And she had gone before Helen could gather herself enough to say goodbye, let alone anything with more substance. It had been an almost ludicrous conversation, with Megan acting as if she was taking away a puppy that Helen was fond of and promising to give it a good home.

Why didn't I attack back? she wondered. Because it wasn't an attack. It was so. . .so *reasonable*, and so sincere!

She had to see Nick. Suddenly this was the only thing that mattered, and she felt that if she could only see him, *now*, she'd be able to talk to him in the right way at last—ask for another chance, ask him to tell her what Megan was giving him that was lacking in their marriage so that she could move heaven and earth herself, if she had to, to provide it. Somehow it helped that he wasn't sleeping with Megan. Nick *was* honourable, as Megan had continued to stress. Surely this physical faithfulness could provide a base on which to build again?

Her lunch hour was ticking away and she had home visits scheduled for the whole afternoon. If she ran a little late she might just have time to drive up to the hospital and find Nick. He had an outpatient clinic due to start any minute. She almost ran back to the health centre car park and was halfway to the hospital before she remembered that her diary and case-notes were still on her desk. She would have to go back for them after she saw Nick and before she could start her home visits.

She wasn't going to go back for them now!

In the outpatient chest clinic a receptionist, whom she didn't know, told her, 'No, Dr Darnell isn't in yet. He's been held back. Are you. . .?' She looked at the name-badge pinned to Helen's dress. 'Oh, *Mrs Darnell?* He's been called to Casualty, Mrs Darnell. I'm not sure what for. Perhaps you can find him there.'

'Thanks. I will.'

Helen hurried down the covered walkway that connected Outpatients to Casualty, which was noisy and frantic following a multiple RTA admission just minutes ago. Directed to a small emergency treatment room tucked towards the back of the large department, Helen found that Nick was caught up completely in an emergency of his own with a cyanosed young man with severe acute asthma stretched out on a bed, a busy nurse and an anxious junior doctor all hovering over him—their words coming in a rapid-fire sequence.

The patient himself seemed so ill that he was scarcely aware of what was happening as he fought grimly for breath, and this was one of those times when a living human body seemed more like a mass of critical chemical reactions than anything else.

'I gave a bolus of 420 mg—' the houseman was saying.

'Hell!' Nick rasped under his breath. 'Did you find out whether he'd taken any orally on his own before he came in?'

'No, I didn't.'

'Next time ask, or at least skip the bolus if you're in doubt and try a steady point nine milligrams per kilogram per hour instead.'

'Right.'

'OK, next. . .' He asked about another drug.

The houseman admitted, 'Not yet.'

'Two hundred and fifty milligrams,' Nick ordered at once, then rasped again, 'Arterial blood gases?'

Helen could only watch, aware that he had not even noticed her as she stood hesitantly just outside the door. He continued to work over the patient for several minutes more, then at last announced, 'Right. That should hold him.' He patted the patient on the shoulder with a gruff encouragement. 'Breathe easy. You're looking better. Relax now. You're responding just as you should. We've got you under the best treatment and observation we possibly can, so please don't be frightened.'

The man's grim and desperate fight against panic and suffocation had eased now. Nick moved away from the bedside, then said to the nurse, 'I'll be back in an hour. Meanwhile, look for a fall in his pulse and respiratory rates and a rise in his peak flow. If you don't see that, then page me. And don't leave him alone. He's scared as hell and that could make him worse.' To the houseman he said, 'Cliff, I want you to stay right on top of those arterial blood gases. That's why we put in the indwelling catheter.'

He launched into a lightning-fast explanation of what the younger doctor should expect to find in the patient's blood gases—and what he should hope *not* to find—and Cliff Runciman narrowed his eyes in concentration and nodded slowly as he tried to take it all in.

'If he's more stable in a couple of hours we'll transfer him upstairs, so check on their bed status, too, would you?'

'How long will you be keeping him in?'

'Several days, I should think. He's still at risk until we can be sure his airflow obstruction is sufficiently reduced, and that's something which can fluctuate unexpectedly. We'll keep him on corticosteroids and full doses of bronchodilators, and measure his peak flow several times a day until it's stable.'

'We'll continue the aminophyllines?'

'Yes, at night, and in a day or two my senior registrar will sit down with him and try to work out what went wrong this time, so he can be better prepared for managing future attacks.' At that moment he caught sight of Helen, who still stood awkwardly just beyond the doorway, and in a changed tone he went on, 'Any clues you or the nursing staff get about what might have triggered this attack, please note them down. And now, if you'll excuse me. . '

He came swiftly out into the corridor. 'Hi!' He looked eager and suddenly expectant. 'So, everything went all right? I've been wondering about it all day.'

For a moment she didn't have a clue what he was talking about, apart from an appalled and miserable thought that he meant her recent interview with Megan. A moment later she dismissed that idea. Even if their marriage was all but over, and he knew all about what Megan had planned to say, he wouldn't approach the subject like this. He saw her blank look and prompted impatiently, 'Liz and the babies. Isn't that why you've come?'

'Oh, of course, yes!' She dragged her fluttering thoughts back to this far happier subject. 'Both boys! Healthy and strong. Pete phoned me over lunch. He sounded exhausted and quite euphoric.'

'Healthy boys! That's marvellous!' His face lit up. 'That's really bloody brilliant for them, after so long. Best adventure of their lives!'

'Adventure?'

'Yes!' He laughed. 'Not the usual kind, you mean? Torrential Amazonian flood-waters and all that? I suppose not, although having to chase Jon down the storm-water drain that time, remember? That came close. Gosh, this brings it all back, doesn't it?'

'It does. . .' she agreed with a smile. Neither Megan nor anyone else could take away their past, and the realisation that Nick could remember it with such happiness on his face gave her a poignant, painful hope.

'Heavens!' he was saying eagerly. 'We must get down to see them as soon as we can.'

'Yes? You want to? Maybe on the weekend?' She responded to the vibrancy and softening in his face, surprised and touched by the strength of his reaction and the palpable evidence of his joy.

She had known that he would be pleased about the news, of course, but hadn't quite expected it to show so much. His grey eyes were sparkling, and he looked a good five years younger as he took her hands in his and squeezed them. 'I have to get over to Outpatients,' he said now. 'Do you have time to walk with me?'

'Um...yes... Yes!' She didn't really—she was already late—but the idea of leaving him immediately seemed impossible.

They set off together, no longer touching but walking in step, and Helen was oblivious to everything but the man at her side. She still felt weak at the knees, thinking of what Megan had said, but her impetuous intention to talk openly about it with him was dissipating by the minute. How could she now, when they had five minutes at the most to spend together?

That scene in the treatment room had frightened and disturbed her too. The level of technical expertise he had displayed as he talked about doses of asthma medication and measurement of arterial blood gases through a catheter left in place as long as necessary was light years beyond her understanding, and brought one of Megan's arguments into ominous focus—Helen could not keep up with Nick in his work. It was true! Of course it was! He had over twenty years of training and practice behind him now. Her own years of nursing training and work as a health visitor didn't even begin to compare.

She had always prided herself in the past that, with her nursing knowledge, she *could* talk to him about his work. She understood how a hospital functioned, she knew the constraints of money and staffing that threatened to restrict him and she even had valuable insights into the social background of some of his patients that he seemed genuinely keen to hear about. But perhaps that was far from being enough.

Arterial blood gases? If he sat down and explained it to her—respiratory acidosis, metabolic alkalosis, base excess--she would certainly grasp the basic principles, but she wouldn't have the ghost of a chance of offering anything useful back to him on the subject.

Did that matter in their marriage? According to Megan, it did.

'Nick,' she said desperately as they reached the walk-way that led to Outpatients.

'Mmm?'

'That patient just then. . .'

'The asthmatic? Terry Preece?'

'Yes. Will he. . .be all right? He seemed pretty ill and you were having to control his treatment very carefully.'

'Yes, acute asthma can be very frightening. I think he'll do well now. It's important not to fall into the trap of assuming the danger's past, that's all. Early discharge or inadequate monitoring could still be fatal. But. . . Is he from your practice? You seem very concerned.'

'No, he's not. It's just. . .'

Hopeless! She didn't know how to talk to him the way Megan did, sprinkling her conversation with speculations about blood carbon dioxide levels or whatever it might be.

'Don't start worrying about my patients,' he teased lightly as they reached Outpatients. 'You've got enough of your own.'

And with that she had to be content. They parted at the door. He swooped in to touch her lips in a light kiss and said again, 'Marvellous news about Liz and Pete. Thanks for coming to tell me,' and of course she couldn't explain that that wasn't why she had come at all.

Dissatisfied and still churned up, she drove impatiently

back to the health centre to pick up her forgotten diary
and notebook and began her home visits. By making a
quick phone call to the first person on her list, she was
able to shuffle that visit to the end of the afternoon and
thus be on time for the rest. She had a relatively routine
series today, including a first visit to a new baby at
the standard age of ten days. The mother was Turkish,
apparently, and spoke very little English. . .

'Hope you don't mind me here, too,' the new father,
Osman Kadir, said in an accent that was pure Yorkshire.
'Arife was nervous and wanted me to interpret, but I
can't stay too long. My brother and I run a Middle Eastern
restaurant, and I have to be there to start cooking by half
past two.'

'Of course I don't mind you here,' Helen told him
with a smile. 'We always like to see a nice, involved
father.'

Osman grinned back. 'The baby's great!'

The couple both stood in the middle of the living-room
of their modest flat, and Helen took in the spotless
cleanliness and beautiful peasant-style décor of Turkish
arts and crafts. The baby boy, Sami, was awake in his
wheeled bassinet, and she clucked and cooed over him
for a little while as she did her usual assessment, again
swept by that disturbingly maternal yearning that Liz's
labour had created in her yesterday. Absurd! She saw
babies like this every day!

Sami Kadir was a dark little creature, healthy but still
too young to have gained the dimpled plumpness that
everyone expected in a baby. There seemed to be no
doubt that he was going to be well loved and well cared
for, but Helen made some notes on a card which she
gave to Osman Kadir and handed him a couple of leaf-
lets as well.

'If your wife is new in England, Mr Kadir, she's probably not aware of the various support services we have.
Here are some things she might like to have a look at—

perhaps you could translate for her? And this leaflet is about immunisations, which you should both talk about together. We do recommend some new ones these days.'

She waited while he spoke in Turkish to Mrs Kadir and the latter nodded several times then began to cough behind her hand, politely and discreetly at first, but then getting to the point where she was clearly distressed about it and she hurried from the room to closet herself in the bathroom with the door tightly closed.

There was an uncomfortable silence, and Osman Kadir frowned.

'Your wife has a cold,' Helen prompted gently, although Arife Kadir hadn't shown any other symptoms of this most mundane of ailments.

'No, she doesn't. . .' he said absently, still frowning at the sounds coming from behind the bathroom door. He paced the room, looking anxious and perplexed. 'She just has a cough. She's had it since we were married.'

'Has she seen anyone about it?' Helen asked him, concealing her alarm. Another case of TB? With a new baby in the house, she hoped not.

'She won't even admit she has it,' Mr Kadir said. He hesitated for a moment, as if wondering whether to trust Helen, then seemed to reach a decision. 'Look, I know you're here about the baby, but—'

'If your wife is ill, that has everything to do with the baby,' Helen pointed out gently. 'That's *really* why I'm here—to make sure that the whole household is functioning and healthy so that the baby has the best chance possible to be healthy, too.'

This seemed to convince the conscientious young husband. 'The thing is,' he plunged in, speaking rapidly now, and glancing frequently at the bathroom door, 'this was an arranged marriage. Arife is my second cousin. Her parents died and she was left alone and badly off, and her uncle wrote to my parents to find out if I'd help by marrying her and bringing her here. I've been in

England since I was ten, but my parents had an arranged marriage and they've always been very happy so. . .you know. . .I have a lot of faith in the old traditions.'

'Your parents must be very pleased about that,' Helen said.

'Yes. Oh, yes. But the thing is, Arife feels she's come empty-handed to the marriage. She was just a factory worker in a cotton mill before she came here—she left school very young—so she didn't have any savings to bring. I've tried to tell her that I love her like anything now. We've been married just over a year, and I got to know her enough in Turkey beforehand to know I liked her. And she's a beautiful girl, a great cook, really bright and funny, too, although she hasn't had much education. I love her!

'But I'm getting really scared, Mrs Darnell. I think she's ill and *she's* too scared to tell me because she thinks I'll send her back. Damaged goods, or something. There could be symptoms other than the cough that she isn't telling me about. She *won't* go to a doctor! We even had a home birth, although I was nervous about that. She says it's allergy, or something stuck in her throat. She often swallows or clears her throat, too, and seems short of breath. I see her trying to hold the cough in, and sometimes I *know* she goes for a walk just so she can cough and I won't hear it.'

There was a click and the bathroom door opened. Dark, slightly built Arife hurried back into the room and said something quickly in Turkish to her husband, who immediately appealed to Helen, 'There! She said it was your perfume.'

'Oh, I'm sorry. . .'

'But it's *not!*'

'Perhaps it is, though, Mr Kadir. In this new environment she could be developing allergies to new substances. Do you notice her struggling with the symptoms at any particular time?'

He thought carefully for a minute. 'Maybe when she's cleaning?'

'Then perhaps it could be an allergy.'

'I just wish she'd *tell* me about it so we can find out and do something. I *know* she knows more than she's telling me!'

He looked across at his wife, who was listening to the conversation uncomprehendingly and looking at Helen with large, frightened eyes. She spoke rapidly again, then Osman said something back to her and she shook her head. He reported to Helen, 'I asked if my sister could come and interpret for her if there was some female stuff she needed to talk about with you. She's fairly traditional about that. She wouldn't let me be in the room during Sami's birth.'

'But she doesn't like the idea of your sister interpreting?'

'No. She says there's nothing to say; everything's fine.' He spread his hands.

Helen left shortly after that, feeling frustrated at not having helped. She wondered whether it would do any good to bring along her own interpreter. Or even a Turkish phrase-book. She jotted down a memo to herself to visit a good bookstore. Not that a phrase-book or dictionary would be enough to facilitate proper conversation but at least it would show that she was trying to reach out, and eventually Arife Kadir might gain enough confidence in her to risk talking about what was on her mind.

Clearly there was something. Was Osman right to think that it had to do with her persistent cough? Or was there something else? Sometimes she had to be content to go very slowly in solving problems that arose with her patients.

Later that afternoon she squeezed in a visit to Barbara James, as last Friday's short talk with Agatha Miller hadn't been very satisfactory. She was hoping for a nice fifteen- or twenty-minute chat—even a cup of tea—but as soon as Barbara met her at the door she knew that this wasn't going to happen.

Barbara was red-eyed and angry. 'No, you can't come in!' She added quickly, 'I'm too cross with Mum! She's just sitting in there as obstinate as an old mule. And the place is a mess! I ducked next door with the kids for five minutes, and when I came back the kitchen was *full* of the smell of cigarette smoke. She wouldn't even admit it at first! And then she said she didn't care. Not care! She's killing herself! I told her I wouldn't have her living here if she wasn't going to at least try!

'She practically set herself on fire the other day, taking her oxygen mask off when she had a lit cigarette in her hand. It flared up and started to burn her fingers. If I hadn't happened to have a glass of cold water in my hand to throw over her. . . How can I go on putting myself out—exhausting myself trying to give her a home to live in—when she thanks me by killing herself in front of my very nose?'

She spilled forth several more emotional sentences, then ended on a tight laugh. 'Sorry! It's a bad day. Do come in. . .and ignore the mess. As for Mum. . .'

In the end they sat in the kitchen and had a productive talk. Helen told Barbara about the first meeting of the emphysema support group, which was now planned for two weeks' time, and suggested that boredom might be part of Mrs Miller's problem. Together they made a list of activities that the elderly woman could do in her handicapped state—things that were pleasurable, as well as household chores such as chopping vegetables while sitting at the kitchen table.

Then Agatha herself laboured into the room and said to her daughter angrily in her wheezing voice, 'You won't let the kids play with me. You tell them it'll make me too tired. But I like playing with them!' and Helen was able to leave with the feeling that things might get better from now on.

The rest of the afternoon was routine, and she arrived home just a few minutes later than usual to run through the familiar mental refrain of, Where are the twins? Are they due home for dinner? No, that's right, they're in London now. Which means it's just me and Nick. How lovely! How lonely! Because Nick and I. . . Nick and I. . .

She made spaghetti Bolognese for dinner and heard his car in the driveway and his key in the door just as it was ready. He looked tired, as usual, and her need to go to him and soothe away the tension in his face with her fingers and her lips was so overwhelming that it felt like far too great a betrayal and she didn't do it, remaining where she stood at the sink to drain the steaming pot of spaghetti into the metal colander.

'How is everything?' she asked him, making her voice bright.

'Fine. I'm thirsty. Hospital's so hot!' And he poured himself a glass of orange juice from the fridge and gulped it down while she grated the cheese and heaped spaghetti and sauce onto their plates. There was silence until, 'How was your day?' he asked.

'Not bad.' It seemed so stilted. Was it true, then, that they didn't talk about their work together because his was too technical for her, and hers was too mundane for him? She thought suddenly of Arife Kadir and her unexplained coughing and said, 'I did come across something this afternoon. . .'

Telling him about it, she knew that she wasn't conveying the scene in the way she wanted to—the caring young husband and the frightened foreign wife, unable to work together on a problem that was starting to strain their marriage.

What was wrong? She always used to be able to talk about her patients in a way that captured his attention, or had seemed to. Now she had doubts. Perhaps, in the past, he was just being polite, and now he no longer bothered. It was always the human angle she emphasised over the scientific one, and now Megan had pointed out that for Nick this wasn't enough. He was a man of science with a complex mind and she couldn't match it.

She could hear herself now, trying to speak dispassion-ately and scientifically about Arife Kadir and her symptoms as Megan might have done, and it was boring and bland and without the technical depth she was reach-ing so hopelessly for and when he said dismissively, 'Sounds like an allergy,' she couldn't really blame him for his lack of interest.

They ate in the dining-room and she was still dwelling on her own inadequacy when he asked, out of the blue, 'Our ward sister on the men's chest ward, Karen Graham—what's your impression of her?'

'Oh. . .' She floundered, so determined to give him what he wanted that she was too absorbed in trying to read his cues to say what she really thought about Karen, which was that she was betraying a dangerous vulner-ability to Paul Chambers's charms. 'She seems competent, caring. . .'

He nodded, clearly dissatisfied, and she went back to thinking about Arife and Osman Kadir. It wasn't just an allergy, she was sure of that. . .

Nick offered to clear up after the meal, and wouldn't listen to her protests. 'You haven't been looking quite yourself tonight, Helen. Take a break. Ring Jon and Jane.'

'No,' she blurted, 'because if I do that, I'll only start worrying about her and Russell again.'

He looked impatient. 'Honestly, Helen, you really mustn't. . .' Then he started to take the empty plates into the kitchen before she'd gathered her thoughts enough to tell him that she really *was* worried about Jane, and could he take it seriously and not dismiss it?

Instead, she wandered restlessly into his study, think-ing, Men are impossible. Nick's impossible. He just doesn't seem to be aware of how ghastly it'll be if they get married. They'll be divorced within two years. But perhaps the idea of divorce didn't worry him any more. . .

He found her still in the study fifteen minutes later and laughed. 'What on earth is this? *Case Studies in Chest Medicine. Principles of Respiratory Medicine.* Heavy stuff, I told you to take a break.'

'Oh, and not bother my pretty little head about things I don't understand?' she snapped at him waspishly, with Megan's well-reasoned accusations drumming in her mind again.

He flinched and turned away as if to hide anger. She wished her shrewish words unsaid at once, of course, but it was too late and her lame apology didn't really clear the air. There was still so much she wanted to say to him, but with a sinking heart she knew that tonight was not the time. The way she was feeling now, any attempt she made to speak frankly about everything that churned inside her would only make things much, much worse.

CHAPTER EIGHT

'HELLO, Karen! How are——?' Helen stopped as the ward sister brushed swiftly past, without a reply, on her way out of Paul Chambers's room. She pulled the particulate respirator from her face as if it was suffocating her and disappeared into the bathroom along the corridor, her feet swift and silent in their rubber-soled nurse's shoes and her abrupt movement punctuated finally by an unheeding slam of the bathroom door.

Helen realised that the question she had started to ask had been unnecessary. It was quite clear how Karen Graham was——terrible! Her eyes were reddened and tear-filled and she was struggling with no success at all against strong emotion.

But what to do about it? She debated going after Karen and forcing her confidence. The ward sister had just been with Paul Chambers, and it didn't take much detective work to realise that she was in tears on his account. Helen soon thought better of the idea, though, and decided to give the younger woman time to calm down and collect herself in private. Perhaps Mr Chambers himself could provide some insight into what was wrong.

She put her own particulate respirator in place and opened the patient's door. A strong draught of air accompanied this action, almost pulling the handle out of her hand. With the fans in his windows set to produce a complete air exchange six times each hour, there was a constant pull of air from the corridor into his room. She closed the door again behind her, and felt the air pressure against it as she did so.

The journalist was standing with his back to her, over by the window, but he wheeled around as soon as he heard the sound of the closing door, and the surprised scowl on his face told her that he had been anticipating Karen Graham's return.

He was in a foul mood, and Helen didn't know how he would have reacted if it had been Karen, but he was definitely not pleased to see *her*! 'What do *you* want?'

'I've just dropped in for a chat,' she told him. 'I had to see a little premmie baby and her mother over in the neonatal unit, so I thought I'd step over here to you as well.' She had come from another visit to Rebecca Minty and her mother, and again was frustrated because the latter still refused to take any break away from her tiny daughter's room.

'Don't give me that!' Paul Chambers growled. 'I've worked out what you're for. You're part of my prescription, just as much as my medicine is. Did that husband of yours write it all down? "Cheerful dose of Helen Darnell, once weekly." You're softening me up, aren't you? Letting me "get used to" you, as if I was a kid or a puppy adjusting to a new babysitter or a kennel, so that when I go home and you come every day to watch me pop my pills I won't bite or throw a tantrum. Well, I don't need to be babied, got it? Now get out!'

'Mr Chambers. . .'

'Did you hear what I said?' His handsome eyes blazed in his leonine face.

'Yes, of course I did.'

'Then do it, if you want me to have any respect left for you. And don't come back!' He went on in a tone that dripped with sarcasm, 'I'll accept your kind visits to my humble abode once I'm discharged, but let's be honest about it, OK? This "dropping in for a chat" is bull, and you know it!'

'Very well, Mr Chambers,' she managed to answer him steadily. 'I'm sorry you feel we've been condescending to you, and I won't visit you in hospital again, since you don't feel it's necessary.'

'Good.' He was still scowling. 'Your husband came to see me this morning. He says I'll be going home next week. I'm no longer sufficiently infectious to warrant hospitalisation, apparently.'

'But that's good news, isn't it?'

'Yes. So why am I in such a foul mood?' He caught the implication in what she *hadn't* said, and characteristically brought it into the open. 'Ask Karen!'

He prowled over to his bed and very deliberately picked up the left-wing news magazine that had been flung onto it. Helen left, not even exerting herself to boom a goodbye through the boxy mask she wore. What an incredibly volatile, difficult man he was! And she *would* ask Karen. She had to now, sensing the crisis that she had feared all along between the patient and the ward sister.

Karen was back at her desk at the nurses' station, head down and pen racing furiously across the paper as she caught up on reports. She was probably very glad, for once, to have the excuse of some paperwork.

'Karen. . .' Helen said carefully, and the pretty blonde ward sister looked up to reveal eyes that were still red and swollen-looking.

'Hi. Is there something I can help you with?'

'I hope so. . .' She saw the defensive expression. Karen knew that she was about to ask about Paul Chambers. After all, what else could it be? He was the only patient she was seeing on this ward at the moment. So there was no point in circling round the subject, or pretending that her question was an innocent one. 'What's going on between you and Mr Chambers?'

Karen didn't bother to prevaricate. Her chin was raised proudly and the spots of colour that Helen had noted a week ago were back, burning on her cheeks. 'I told him he must stop sending me flowers, and he told me he wouldn't.'

'Flowers?'

'Yes, to the flat I share with some friends. Gifts, too. He's angry because I give them to charity. And I'm angry because—!' She broke off, then continued helplessly, staring down at her hands now. 'He wants me to move into his house to be waiting for him when he's discharged. He won't respect the fact that I'm trying to keep a professional distance while he's still my patient. He says this thing is too strong between us to resist, and he's right but...he should be helping me maintain my role, not...not doing this to me!'

'Could you ask for a transfer to another ward?' Helen suggested. The poor girl was distraught, and it was obvious that a powerfully sexual, manipulative man like Paul Chambers was totally beyond her experience and her ability to deal with.

'No... No, I couldn't do that,' she said distractedly, her colour coming and going wildly. 'I— He needs me here too much. And I need him. All we have to do is wait...' She stared into space for a minute with a set jaw, then refocused and said, 'Dr Darnell is discharging him some time next week if his next culture is as good as this week's was. Did you know?'

'Yes, Paul told me,' Helen managed, then added very seriously, 'Look, Karen, if you need to talk this is my number at work, and this is my home number.' She pulled a sheet of paper across and scribbled the numbers down. 'Don't let that home number get into general circulation, will you, or Nick will be besieged with calls? But do ring, at any time, if you need to.'

'Thanks, Mrs Darnell.' Karen smiled tightly. 'I appreciate that. Believe me, this has all ambushed me out of the blue. But it'll work out, and it has to be right. That's all I know. Feeling like this...it *will* work out!'

She seemed calm and quite radiant suddenly, and Helen wondered as she said a brief goodbye and left the ward, Could it work? Could it be the making of both of them?

Perhaps. So utterly different from her relationship with Nick, though. Theirs had always been a marriage of trust and equality in giving, she had considered, while Karen would be embarking on a partnership where one gained and the other sacrificed, perhaps with little in the way of thanks. Did she fully realise that? It would be ironic if it did work, Helen decided, even while her own marriage was floundering in a state where shared giving no longer seemed to do the trick.

It was Friday afternoon, and she had specially arranged her visits here at the hospital for the end of the day so that directly afterwards she could go up to Nick's office, tucked away at the back of the oldest hospital building, and collect him. They were then driving straight down to see Liz and Pete and the new boys, who had been brought home from the hospital just yesterday.

They planned to eat on the way, knowing that the last thing the new parents needed was to be cooking and serving for guests. Helen was bringing two frozen casseroles as well, which she had made earlier in the week, to be thawed and eaten on nights when Liz simply couldn't manage to get a meal on the table.

With the abrupt termination of her visit to Paul Chambers, though, Helen was a little early as she climbed the echoing stairs to Nick's second-floor office, and when she knocked on the door no one answered. Nick shared a secretary with Tony Glover, the other consultant thoracic physician at Camberton Hospital, and kindly, efficient Mrs Pepworth worked for the latter on Friday afternoons. Helen could hear her typewriter clattering in the office across the hall.

But Nick's door wasn't locked, she found when she tried the handle. She went in and looked on his desk for a message, in case something unexpected had come up, but there was nothing there—only a book on occupational lung diseases, with a very bilious green cover which seemed to befit the subject matter of the book rather too well. She stared at it absently, wondering what to try next. A phone call to Outpatients, or Casualty, in case he was there?

Then she heard his voice down the corridor. 'I agree that in many ways it would be practical to go apartment-hunting in Boston together, Megan, but I don't think it would be appropriate.' He spoke very steadily. 'We may decide on two entirely different areas of the city. Besides, it's not definitely decided yet that Helen is staying behind, and if she does come—'

'She wants to stay behind, though,' Megan interrupted eagerly. 'The twins, her job. . . Boston's expensive. It might even turn out to make sense if we—'

'Let's not discuss it now, if you don't mind.' He sounded very tired.

'Well, we'll see, then, shall we?' was Megan's firm conclusion. 'Things change, after all. . .'

Occupational lung diseases. Occupational lung diseases. Helen felt as if she had one. Her chest was tight and her breathing was painful, and in another few seconds. . . Yes! Nick and Megan appeared in the doorway, both looking startled and uncomfortable at seeing her there. Some of the coffee that Nick carried in the frivolous mug she had given him several years ago splashed onto his hand and he muttered an expletive between clenched teeth.

Megan was flushing. She wore her scarlet suit again and it made her look impossibly tall and poised, although now she seemed to be ducking her head in an awkward gesture.

'Hello, Helen. . .' She had spoken the greeting before Nick did. 'You're early.'

'Oh, you knew what time I was expected, did you?' Helen's tone was mild but her fists were clenched, though neither of them were able to see beyond the edge of the desk where she still stood.

'Yes,' Megan said brightly. 'Nick mentioned you were

going down to visit some old friends who've had twins.'

And Helen, who had been looking forward to the trip, suddenly saw it through Megan's eyes as a duty call and nothing more—something Nick might have tried to get out of if he could. She said quickly, 'It looks as if you've both still got work to do. I'll go and get a coffee, too, if you don't mind.' She was familiar with the little kitchenette down the corridor.

'This can wait,' Nick growled.

'No, no.' Bright, not meeting his eye. 'Because we've told Liz and Pete seven-thirty or later, and they wouldn't thank us for getting there early.'

'True. OK, then.' He turned at once to his senior registrar, his strong, lean hand spread absently on the bilious green book cover that had carved itself into Helen's memory. 'Now, back to what we were talking about before. . . Megan you want to read Shultz, Felton and Hansen on allergy to spores of. . .'

Helen let herself out quietly, hoping for a smile from Nick just before she closed the door between them, but those grey eyes she loved so much were staring down at the book, now opened, on his desk. 'Here's the reference. . .'

She made her coffee and drank it without a single sip of pleasure, standing in the cramped space of the kitchen. If Megan felt confident enough of Nick's feelings for her to suggest apartment-hunting together in Boston, with the distinct possibility hovering in the air of deciding to share. . . Nick had said no to the idea, hadn't wanted to discuss it today, but if Megan pursued the thing relentlessly, as Paul Chambers was relentlessly pursuing Karen Graham. . .

What was it about these modern young women: prepared to live with a man after knowing him a month; making propositions to married men about apartment-sharing, and refusing to accept that the subject was closed? Helen felt old, and at sea, and quite convinced that she had already lost the battle.

Nick came and found her after about fifteen minutes.
'Ready?'

'Yes.' She flung the last inch of her coffee down the
sink and rinsed out the cup.

'You didn't have to exile yourself in here, you know,'
he told her gently, not meeting her eye. 'Our discussion
was tedious and technical, but not confidential.'

'Technical? Oh, then I wouldn't have understood a
word of it, and my mediocre brain would have been
bored,' she said waspishly.

He frowned uneasily. 'Helen. . .'

And she glowered at him, unrepentant.

They were silent in the car and when they stopped for
a quick meal in a cosy pub it might have been very
pleasant, except that all they managed to discuss was
the menu. He ate hungrily, scarcely pausing for breath
between the neat mouthfuls, and she accused, 'You forgot
to have lunch.'

'I didn't forget. I didn't have time. This is delicious,
though!'

'Yes, so's mine.'

When they resumed their journey Nick insisted on
driving again, although she could see how tired he was.
His eyes had that creased look that she always longed to
kiss away, and she knew that there was always a spot in
his neck that burned by the end of a long week. She had
massaged it countless times in the past, and her hands
suddenly tingled with a need to touch him there—to
feel the tight, strong muscles soften and become supple
beneath her kneading movements.

At the same time she was furious with him—he should
have been firmer with Megan—in an illogical way that
made her sift through every disagreement or misunder-
standing they'd ever had and read enormous significance
into it. Tears pinched in her eyes, and she turned to stare
out of the window, hoping that he wouldn't see, and, at

the same time—this really made sense—desperate for him to notice, stop the car and take her into his arms.

At first her mind seethed with rehearsed speeches to him and there were moments when the words almost burst forth, but there must have been a shred of sanity left in her because she managed to see clearly that now, feeling like this, would be the worst time in the world to talk to him about everything that had been going wrong lately. It would come out as shrewish accusations, or illogical storms of need and pain, and if she brought Megan's name into it she was afraid that she would say things that would alienate him hopelessly for ever.

Instead, she tried to distract herself by thinking about something sensible, but all that came to mind was that book on his desk about occupational lung diseases. She began to plot out the work week that followed this weekend. Three immunisation clinics, two visits to schools, a big practice meeting on Monday, single mothers' group, home visits. Was Agatha Miller cutting down on her smoking? How was Arife Kadir managing with new baby Sami? Arife Kadir. Occupational lung diseases.

'Byssinosis!' It came out so abruptly that it sounded like a sneeze, and Nick looked so startled that she almost laughed aloud.

'What?' he barked, as his attention veered wildly between her and the road.

'Mr Kadir said she worked in a factory after leaving school at thirteen. I'm pretty sure he said a cotton mill. Turkey produces lots of cotton, doesn't it?'

'Yes, I believe so, but who—?'

'Arife Kadir. That new mother I tried to tell you about the other day with the mysterious symptoms that she won't talk about to her husband.'

'I remember. It sounded like an allergy.'

'But it could be byssinosis, couldn't it? Cotton worker's disease?' She was eager, but his response was slow and careful.

'It's possible. Not likely, though. She's young, isn't she?'

'Twenty-four, I think.'

'And you say she started working in the mill at thirteen?'

'Yes.'

'Eleven years' exposure to cotton dust. Byssinosis can occur after that length of time but she's not in a Turkish cotton mill any more, she's here.'

'Can't byssinosis become chronic to the point where the symptoms are present even when there's no longer any exposure?' She was almost pleading, so desperate to have him take her seriously—as seriously as he would have taken Megan, she was certain, if the other woman had suggested the same thing.

'Again, yes, it can happen,' he conceded. 'Unusual in someone so young.'

'Osman Kadir said he thought it got worse when she was cleaning. Now, if her cleaning includes dusting and vacuuming, or maybe even beating rugs... They had some lovely Turkish things there—rugs and wall-hangings and woven cotton drapes—and I saw a big basket of craft-work, too, with spools of cotton yarn. Surely—!'

'Helen, you can't ask me to diagnose byssinosis in a patient I haven't even seen!'

'You'll have to see her, then. I wonder if I can get her to come in to your outpatients' clinic. I was going to get a phrase-book and a dictionary, try to talk to her myself... She must know! She must know that it's byssinosis and she's afraid Osman won't want her because she has a chronic illness. If it *was*...'

'Helen—'

'Just say it was, Nick, what would you do to treat it? There's surely no need for her to be so concerned. You could alleviate the symptoms, couldn't you?'

'Oh, yes, with bronchodilators. If she was still working

in a mill there are some other drugs which would be appropriate as well, but in this case we'd hope that with time and no further exposure the symptoms would decrease and an inhaled bronchodilator would be enough. But, Helen—'

'I know, Nick. I know I'm jumping to conclusions, but don't you think it's likely enough that you should at least *see* her—if I can get her to agree to it?'

'Sure, yes. It certainly sounds like my territory. Possibly it could be ordinary asthma that's never been diagnosed, perhaps exacerbated by stress, or some irritant present in her new environment. And, of course, there are other respiratory problems that can present with those symptoms. We'd have to do an exercise challenge test, measure her peak flow and see if that cough is actually producing anything, which would put a whole new light on her condition. . .'

'You see, it's interesting, isn't it?' she said to him, hearing the beseeching note in her voice. 'Here's this young woman, who may even know already exactly what is wrong with her but for all sorts of personal and cultural reasons she's not admitting it. That's why I think my job's worthwhile, Nick, even though I don't have a tenth of your depth of knowledge, and can't talk about it in the way Megan can. I need to know about *people* and to pick up on the clues I get when I visit them at home, and that's valuable and satisfying.'

He glanced across at her, amazement colouring his face. 'Well, of course, darling. That's why I value your insights so much when there's a patient we share. Gosh, if you jawed on and on about lung function and so on, I'd start to think I had a research assistant instead of a wife.'

'You mean that?' she asked quietly.

'Of course! My God, has it been bothering you— has it?'

'Megan said—'

'For heaven's sake, let's leave Megan out of this, shall

we?' he growled ominously. 'We have to deal with what's between you and me, Helen.'

But Megan *is* between you and me, she wanted to cry out. She didn't, though. And then she remembered Megan's insistence on Nick's decency—that he wouldn't get involved with another woman until he was officially separated from his wife. Was that what he was implying now? That the problems in their marriage were purely their own fault, with no convenient third party to blame? He was probably right. Focusing on Megan as the interloper was only stopping Helen from addressing the real issues.

Controlling herself, she said carefully, 'I have been worried lately that I couldn't match your knowledge; couldn't act as a sounding board for you about your work, and this might matter more in Boston than it does here because there'll be more research and less patient contact.'

There was a small silence, as he seemed to weigh her words. 'That's true, of course, but really, Helen, it doesn't matter. I'd far rather have your warmth, your— Damn it, when I think of Paul Chambers and how quickly you put your finger on what makes him tick. . .'

'Then. . .then you think I was right about him?'

'Oh, yes! I admit it seemed far-fetched at first. Megan's opinion made more sense on paper—he's an intelligent man, he understands the issues and he'll comply fully with his treatment from now on. But seeing him over the past week and what he's doing to poor Karen. . .'

'Oh, you know about that? And you think it's deliberate?'

'I'm sure of it. She'd be damned useful to him, and he knows she hasn't had the experience of life to resist such a relentlessly romantic, machismo assault on her heart. She's swept away on a tide of starry-eyed passion, and sincerely believes he feels the same.'

'She was in tears today,' Helen said. 'She's trying

desperately to maintain her professionalism, but can't help talking about his ''need'' for her. She's like a moth beating its wings against the glass to get to the light. I even wondered if it might work for them. If they'd each fulfil the other's needs and be happy.'

'No,' he answered decisively, 'Paul Chambers couldn't make any woman happy. You're still a romantic, aren't you?'

'No. . . I used to be. . .' She stifled the sigh that threatened to punctuate the comment and managed a dry laugh instead but Nick was silent. Unable to bear this, she searched for something else in her work day that might interest him, and remembered Freda and tiny Rebecca Minty. She sketched the background of their story briefly, then finished, 'I'm sure she's heading for complete nervous exhaustion.'

But he laughed and she instantly resented it, then calmed down as he said, 'I'm thinking of you when the twins were born. Do you remember? When they were in the special care nursery?'

'As if I'd forget!'

'And I was wringing my hands. I had a heart-to-heart with my obstetrics professor and he told me not to worry. He said you'd pace yourself as you needed to, and he was right. The day before they were due home you suddenly seemed to realise that if they were going to be discharged then they must be healthy, and it was *probably* safe to actually get some rest. You conked out for fifteen hours straight, if I remember.'

'Did I? I'd forgotten. . . But that's right, I was so full of milk when I woke up that I was afraid I'd explode! And you never told me about the heart-to-heart with Professor Blackstone! I thought you were all terrified of him!'

'We were but I had a courage born of desperation that week, and I thought if I'd lived through seeing you in the pain of labour I could live through anything—even him.'

'Idiot!' she laughed.

He went on more seriously, 'Now, from what you've said, little Rebecca isn't going to be home for weeks yet.'

'No, she's doing well now, but she still has a huge amount of growing to do.'

'Then don't worry about Mrs Minty. She has an instinct for her baby's well-being, and that can't be bad.'

'Yes, and some mothers have the opposite problem with their premmie babies. They're distanced by all the technology and don't manage to form a bond as soon as they should.'

'So give her a few more weeks and if she still hasn't relaxed, then you can start to worry.'

'Mmm, I think you're right. . . And I'm amazed that you still remember how long I slept the day before Jon and Jane came home!'

The lights of the Holloways' mill loomed ahead, and Helen felt somewhat better than she had at the start of the journey. The air between them had cleared a little, a very little. At least Megan had been proved wrong about one thing—Nick *didn't* mind that she couldn't match his medical knowledge, and this fact gave her the courage to work on everything else.

As they got out of the car he chuckled, 'Oh-oh, hear that sound?'

Helen listened, and heard it too. A baby crying. No, two of them. 'Oh, dear. . .'

Liz was in tears and Pete was helpless. 'We don't know what to do! Thank God you've come! We were just about to ring our GP.'

Nick stepped forward with a wry smile. 'Hey, who's this noisy monster? Stephen? Hello, little lad. This is your Uncle Nick here. . .' He took the tiny red-head with a gentleness and deftness that had him out of Liz's arms before she even realised what was happening, and his voice was soft and lilting. 'Now, then. . .' He lifted the baby onto his shoulder, patting his back and bouncing him gently. 'What's going on, hey?'

Helen slipped past to take little Christopher from Pete but Liz had already reached for him, glaring at her husband as if she suddenly didn't trust him with his new son. Both of them were clearly at the end of their tether.

'I had two lectures to give, so I was out all the afternoon,' Pete said miserably. 'Everything was fine before I left but Liz says they've been like this since two o'clock, and we haven't got a clue what's wrong.'

'Nothing's wrong,' Nick said. 'They're just being babies.'

For a moment the two new parents looked at him as if he'd failed every medical exam he ever took. This man? A doctor? Impossible! He was a sadist and a fool!

'You mean we have to live with this until they *stop* being babies?' Pete almost shrieked. 'It can't be right. They must be in pain. It *must* be something. They must be feverish. . .'

'I didn't mean you'd have to live with it,' Nick laughed. 'Sorry. Bad way to put it. I just meant it's probably something upsetting their little systems, and with a baby it doesn't take much to do that. Liz, how's your diet? Could there be anything iffy in your milk?'

'My diet's textbook perfect,' she wailed. 'I'm a walking advertisement for the four basic food groups, but you know what—it's not doing a thing for *my* ''system'', either. I've been drinking prune juice until I'm drowning in it.'

'Oh. . .' said Helen.

'Ah!' said Nick. 'That's it, then.'

'Prune juice?'

'Yes, try high-fibre tablets and lots of plain water instead from now on. I'd say their little pipes are all-a-gurgle. Aren't they, little man? Hey? You've got the intestinal collywobbles!'

Nick was still bouncing and patting Stephen, whose cries had subsided considerably now. Helen couldn't take her eyes off him. His whole face had softened and his tiredness seemed to have quite gone. He held the swaddled, football-sized bundle with a mixture of care and tenderness which had returned to him instantly, a body-memory from eighteen years ago when Jon and Jane were newly born. He had been good at it then. Now, there was an added maturity to him that made the picture even more poignantly sweet to her eyes.

He knows, now, how fast they grow, she realised. He's enjoying every second of this because next time we see the babies they'll already be different.

Stephen had stopped crying now, and Christopher's sounds were just soft grumblings. Nick grinned with satisfaction—and not a little smugness, to be honest—and nuzzled the tiny little head that lay on his shoulder with his cheek very softly, so as not to fret the satiny skin with his new growth of dark stubble.

'I don't believe it!' Liz whispered. 'He's going to sleep. Did you hypnotise him, Nick?'

'Takes years of medical training,' he told her soberly. 'Honestly, I can't begin to explain how it's done!'

She laughed and sobbed at the same time. 'I hate you! And will you both stay here for ever and ever and be nannies?'

'They sense your emotions, you see,' Nick explained just as Helen could have done, except that she was so much enjoying listening to him and watching him. His voice was low and quiet, lilting and soothing. 'They were tired and frazzled and so were you, and you were all making each other worse. That's right, isn't it, little man? Do skip the prune juice and try the bouncing and patting. Almost all babies love to be up on a shoulder for some reason—probably to prevent their parents from getting any rest—and preferably with you standing and pacing the room, thanks very much!'

'Lying them on their tummies across your knees and

gently rocking your legs from side to side can work, too,'
Helen came in.

'Or letting them kick on a bunny rug on the floor with
their nappy off a couple of times a day,' Nick suggested.

'Pushing their knees gently against their tummies, and
pulling their legs straight again.'

'Sometimes they just want to nurse for an hour or two
at a stretch for comfort during fussy times.'

'Putting them face down in the bassinet and thumping
them rhythmically on their nappied bottoms. . .'

'Stop!' Pete was covering his ears. 'Can we write all
this down?'

'It'll come to you in no time,' Helen promised him.
'Within another week or two you'll be the greatest
experts in the world on your own babies, and what works
and what doesn't.'

'Two weeks? If we live that long!' Liz groaned.

'But your mother is coming on Monday, Liz,' Pete
pointed out.

'I know, but she said on the phone that she'd forgotten
everything she ever knew about it,' Liz said gloomily.

'So had I,' Nick said in a cheerful whisper. Stephen
was sleeping noisily on his shoulder, as snuffly as a
little pig.

'No, you hadn't,' Helen told him, unable to keep the
tenderness from her voice.

'You should have another one, you two,' Pete said,
struck with the inspirational idea. 'Honestly, it was the
best moment of my life. This has been the best week of
my life.' And somehow they all knew that it was true,
in spite of his haggard appearance and recent despair.

'You *should*!' agreed Liz.

Helen looked at Nick, scarcely daring to hope. . . He
was hesitating, his mouth opened slightly and the tip of
his tongue resting against his top lip. 'Ah. . . I think we're
past all that, aren't we, Helen?' he said, glancing at her,
his tone carefully light as if he didn't want to hurt Liz's

feelings. 'It wouldn't be at all sensible to start all over again.'

'No, it wouldn't,' Helen managed, trying to mean it. 'Not sensible at all.'

CHAPTER NINE

'HOPE it's not too early to ring!' Jane sounded very chirpy on the phone the following Thursday morning, a dourly rainy one.

'No, of course it isn't,' Helen told her, experiencing the usual surge of pleasure at hearing her daughter's voice, coupled with an automatic unworded question—there's nothing wrong, is there? 'I do have to leave for work in a few minutes. . .' And most of her breakfast was still sitting on the kitchen bench, uneaten. But that didn't matter. She still missed the twins badly, and would happily sacrifice breakfast for a talk.

'I know,' Jane said. 'I'll be quick. Just wanted to check that you are coming down this weekend.'

'I was going to ring you tonight about it.'

'I thought you might, and Jon and I have a party to go to. . .'

'A party? On a Thursday?'

'Yes, Mum, on a Thursday,' Jane sighed with heavy patience. 'People's birthdays do come on Thursdays sometimes, you know.'

'Do they really, you cheeky thing?'

'No, but I know what you mean,' Jane added repentantly. 'And, yes, I *am* studying. Ask me anything in the universe about invertebrates, and I can probably at least tell you what book to look it up in!'

'Good, and, yes, we are coming on the weekend—just a flying visit. Your dad can't leave till after he's seen a couple of patients first thing Saturday morning. We're going to take the train, and we've booked a bed and breakfast quite near you. We'll leave our things there and then get to you in the early afternoon.'

'I think Jon will be out. *With a girl*, actually.'

'Oh, no, not another engagement in the wind, getting in the way of your studies,' Helen blurted unwisely. This business of having children who thought they were grown up—and possibly even were—was distinctly unnerving at times.

There was a short, pregnant silence at the other end of the phone. Then, 'Yes, well, we won't talk about that now, Mum.'

'No. . .'

She remembered all Nick's warnings about not lecturing or nagging Jane. Sensible? Maybe. Impossible, though! Nick had already left for work and for a moment she was tempted to say, 'Yes, *do* let's talk about it now!' But something stopped her—a half-unwilling acknowledgement of Nick's innate sense and tact in his relationship with Jane.

If he was here now, listening to her end of the conversation, he'd be frowning at her and signalling 'No!' with those expressive grey eyes that she loved so much and was so afraid of losing. And, yes, perhaps he'd be right, she conceded to herself unwillingly.

'Dying to see you both,' she said instead, meaning it but meaning Jon and Jane.

Her daughter took it the other way. 'Um. . . You might not see Russell. He's pretty busy.'

'Well, I meant Jon, actually.'

'Oh, of course.'

'So, bye-bye for now, darling.'

'Bye, Mum. Love you, old duckie, I do!'

And, spluttering slightly at that last outrageous endearment, Helen put down the phone—untouched by any premonition about Jane's engagement or anything else.

She had a busy morning at the health centre, spending much of her time on the phone scheduling tests for some of her patients, including a hearing test for a ten-month-old who didn't seem quite on target developmentally for her age.

On Monday she had succeeded in persuading Arife Kadir to attend Nick's clinic this afternoon, and she rang the Turkish woman's husband to remind him and stress its importance.

'I won't be able to be there myself,' she said, 'but I've told my husband everything you told me about her work in the cotton mill. As long as you'll be there, Mr Kadir. . .'

'I will,' he assured her. 'And my sister's helping Kemal in the restaurant this afternoon in case we run late at the clinic.'

'Good.'

There was a fair bit of work to do to prepare for Monday's first emphysema support group meeting too. Stella Harris was enthusiastic in her involvement and the other nurses in the practice, Marcella McPherson, Anne Robson and Delia Cross, had each come up with some patients who they were encouraging to attend.

Immediately before lunch Helen made her second visit to Paul Chambers at home. He had been discharged on Tuesday, and she had supervised his drug-taking yesterday morning as well. She had been thankful that there was no evidence of Karen Graham in his untidy terrace cottage. Although no longer actively infectious, he was still far from being cured and her daily visits to him would continue for months more—well into next year, in fact, when Nick would be in Boston.

Making this connection depressed her, and she wasn't looking forward to seeing the recalcitrant Mr Chambers. He had managed to drag out her visit yesterday so that she was late for the rest of the morning. It should only have taken five minutes, and so these delaying tactics couldn't be allowed to continue.

Today she'd left a cushion of time by fitting him in right before her lunch-hour, but she wasn't prepared to let him encroach on that too much, either. After all, she was only there to watch him take his pills, and much of the time he seemed determined to show that he didn't even like her.

Already on edge, she knocked on his door, glancing down the row of attractively renovated workers' terrace cottages to Stella's place two doors away. The contrast was immediately apparent. Stella had worked energetically to make her small square of front garden bright and attractive, even in today's light rain, while Paul's displayed only straggly lawn and beds of luxuriant weeds. Well, to be fair, he'd been in hospital for a month, hadn't he?

The inside of the house was in a similar state, however, as she had noted the other day, and if it hadn't improved in a few days once he got himself settled she would try to suggest, tactfully, that he employ a cleaner part-time if he couldn't or wouldn't do it himself. He still wasn't in a position where he could afford any secondary infections due to poor hygiene.

Scuffling footsteps, a bump and the sound of low, male swearing came from inside and then the door was opened. Paul Chambers stood there with his face still rumpled from sleep, wearing only a green towelling dressing-gown which gaped across his broad, barrel-like and thickly haired chest. Helen was taken aback, although she had encountered people even less prepared for her visits many times. He picked up on it immediately, of course, and grinned attractively, then scratched his stomach and ran his powerful hand through his bronze and grey mane of hair.

'Come in, Mrs Darnell, do!'

She did, and was immediately struck by the change in the small sitting-room—freshly vacuumed, boxes of papers tidied to some other part of the house, bright flowers on the mantelpiece, every exotically lovely ornament perfectly placed and lovingly dusted and no longer the empty pizza box and Chinese food containers piled onto the coffee table. The difference from yesterday was so marked that the reason for it seemed horribly obvious. . .

'I'll get my pills,' he said briefly. 'They're in the bathroom, I think.'

'You left them in one of the kitchen cupboards yesterday,' she pointed out.

But he was already on his way up the stairs and flung back casually at her, 'Karen tidied them away.'

Helen's heart sank. So it *had* happened!

And then Karen Graham herself appeared on the stairs, receiving Paul's rough caress as he passed her before coming steadily down to greet Helen. She, too, wore a dressing-gown, an exotic silk smoking jacket that looked far too big for her and must be Paul's. It slipped off her shoulder and she pulled at it as she said calmly, 'Hello, Mrs Darnell. You don't have to stay. I'll make sure he takes them.'

'I can't let you do that, Karen, and you know it,' Helen answered reproachfully. 'This is my job. You're here—'

'In a purely personal capacity?' the plumply pretty nurse finished, her smile wryly crooked. She lifted her chin, those bright spots of colour in her cheeks. 'You're shocked and disapproving, I suppose.'

'No, not that,' Helen answered slowly. 'Although I suppose I hoped you'd think about it more carefully before you took such a step.'

'I have thought about it. I've done nothing *but* think about it for several weeks. It's what I want.'

'Then that's all that needs to be said, isn't it?'

'*I* think so. My parents. . .weren't of the same opinion.'

'I can't find them, Karen, damn you; where the hell did you put them?' came Paul's voice, exploding violently down the stairs.

She seemed unperturbed at his tone, and looked

flushed and calm and happy. 'They're in the cabinet, right next to your shaving things,' she called back. 'Shall I get some coffee on?'

'God, yes!'

Turning to Helen again, she said, 'I know you have to do your job for now, but I might as well tell you we won't be here more than a few weeks longer.'

'Not here?'

'We're going to Morocco. I'll be giving my notice in at the hospital tomorrow. I'm on days off at the moment. You see, now that winter's on its way we want to be somewhere dry and sunny and warm, for the sake of his lungs. There's been some permanent damage done to them, as you know, and he needs to be strong enough to work on his book. His editor wants it by early in the new year. Don't worry, I'm not going to let him get away with missing his dose. I'll make sure he eats properly, too. I don't want to lose him to this disease, or to anything else!'

'I hope you'll be happy, then, Karen,' Helen said inadequately, recognising that no kind of argument or persuasion would be of the slightest use. Her heart went out to Karen's parents, wherever they were, as she thought, How would I feel if this were Jane?

And yet. . .and yet. . . She could glimpse what Karen saw in the man—his rough, knowing good looks, his cynical intelligence, the aura of exotic places and adventures that clung to him like some potent dust. Karen was responding to him as she might have responded to a compelling book—lost, entranced, swept away.

That flush, so often glowing on her face, was reminiscent of the hectic colour that TB patients often had in the later stages of the disease, and it was as if Karen had contracted a disease just as real as TB—the disease of a wild, heedless infatuation. Possibly even love. How could Helen say? But thinking this way reminded her that Paul himself really *was* ill.

'Be careful,' she told Karen. 'His sputum culture was good enough to discharge him but it wasn't completely negative yet, was it?'

'No. Dr Darnell felt that, since he lived alone and wasn't in contact with any small children or elderly people, there was no risk.'

'But he's not living alone now, is he?' Helen pointed out gently. 'He's living very intimately with you. If you ever have the slightest suspicions of symptoms. . .'

'I'll look after myself,' Karen answered steadily. 'After all, I wouldn't be much use to him if I was ill, would I?'

Paul reappeared with his clutch of pill bottles in hand, and Helen went into the kitchen with them both—it was also spotlessly clean and neat—and watched him fling pills down his throat, gag a little, chew and gulp water while Karen put on a rich brew of Greek coffee.

'Will you stay for a cup, Mrs Darnell?'

'I can't. I have home visits to make,' Helen said, not quite truthfully as it was her lunch-hour that loomed in the immediate future.

'Well, we'll see you tomorrow, then.'

Helen left as the smell of coffee began to fill the small cottage. She had been planning to eat her sandwiches in the car, but she felt drained and disturbed by Karen's presence in Paul Chambers's house—even though she had sensed the other day that it had been inevitable—and decided to go back to the health centre, not far away, where she could grab a cup of tea and shake off her helpless concern for Karen.

Jane's engagement to Russell Baldwin paled by comparison and she realised, with a blinding flash of clear understanding, Nick has been right about it all along, and I shouldn't have been angry with him about it. Jane's a sensible girl, and she's a long way from being married yet. Compared with what Karen is doing, living with an egocentric and self-destructive man nearly twenty years her senior whom she's known for just over a month, throwing away her nursing career and her family and her friends for some exotic artistic exile in Morocco. . . I should have confidence in my daughter's judgement. . . and my husband's!

But her tea was destined to remain undrunk. The phone rang on her desk just as she had taken the first sip, and she heard Barbara James's worried voice at the other end of the line. 'Mrs Darnell? Oh, good! Look, I didn't know who to ring. Mum's not too good but she doesn't want to come in and see anyone. She's being impossible, really! Stubborn as an old. . . Anyway, should I insist? Or ring Dr Anderson? The children are sick, too, with colds. That's what Mum says she's got but she's fighting for every breath and. . . Anyway, so I don't really want to drag the children out in this rain. . .'

'Would you like me to drop in?' Helen offered. 'I'll be over that way later on so I could come to you beforehand, within the next half-hour.'

'Would you?' Barbara's eagerness told Helen that this was what she had been hoping for.

She ended the phone conversation quickly, surrendered the tranquillity of having the office to herself as she drank her tea and went straight out to the car, taking her well-travelled packet of sandwiches with her. She managed to eat half of one on the way as she drove.

At the Jameses' house, Barbara met her at the door. 'Thank goodness! She's got worse even since I phoned. She's lying down. Come through.'

Agatha Miller lay in the darkened dining-room which had been converted to make a bedroom for her. She was breathing heavily through her venturi mask and, when Helen asked Barbara to draw the curtains so that she could see the elderly woman in a better light, she saw the bluish colour around her lips and fingers.

'What symptoms has she been complaining of?' Mrs Miller herself looked drowsy and unable to reply.

'She's had a headache the past few mornings, and she says her ankles are swollen. I told her that was because she's not moving round enough.'

'Can I have a look?'

'I'll try and get her to sit up. Mum? Mum? Mrs Darnell needs you to sit up.'

With a combination of coaxing and physical effort, Mrs James got her mother into a sitting position and Helen saw that her ankles were indeed very puffy. Barbara was watching her, anxious and yet clearly waiting for a reassurance that it was nothing serious and she could continue to look after her mother at home. Unfortunately, this wasn't the case. Helen had recognised the symptoms of respiratory failure, and the ankles' swelling suggested that partial heart failure was developing as well—although only a doctor would be able to establish this for certain.

'I'm afraid your mother needs to be admitted straight away,' she told Mrs James, after moving out of the patient's room.

'Oh, no! Oh, my goodness!' Barbara blinked back some shocked tears. 'She's dying, isn't she?'

'Not yet. . . Except in the sense that she's been dying for a long time already, as you know. . .'

'It's those foul cigarettes, and she *won't* give them up! Oh, I'm so angry with her!' Barbara was really crying now. 'I so much wanted to have her here, but it's not working out, is it? She won't be able to come back?'

'I doubt it,' Helen said with gentle honesty. 'We were hoping for a little more co-operation from her, weren't we?'

'What will happen, then?'

'A period of hospital care, as before, and then a residential setting, with professional help close at hand. In many ways it'll be easier on her and on you and your family.'

'I'd better get the children dressed, then. They're

both in bed, too, quite under the weather. . .'

Helen thought quickly, then said, 'I can take her. Or I can call an ambulance.'

'No, not that, please, unless you really have to. It'll panic her. Those sirens really spell death to her when she hears one.'

'Then I'll take her myself. If I can just make a couple of quick phone calls. . .'

It was by no means the first time Helen had had to shuffle her home visits at short notice. Mrs Miller, surprisingly, did not put up the expected fight about going back into hospital, and Helen felt that this was a symptom in itself of how ill she was. She seemed confused for several minutes, asking who would feed the cat—as if she still lived alone in her own place—and then she was worried about Helen driving what she clearly thought was her son-in-law's car when, in fact, of course, it was the health service vehicle that Helen used in her work.

Barbara had hastily packed a bag of her mother's things and said, as she bent down to Mrs Miller in the passenger seat, 'I'll be along to visit tonight, Mum, and if I've forgotten anything, I'll bring it then.'

But Mrs Miller didn't reply, too intent on drawing air into her lungs from the portable oxygen equipment that Helen had arranged on the floor of the car in front of her patient.

Phoning ahead, Helen had arranged a bed and Nick's senior house officer, Colin Hart, came immediately to listen to the elderly woman's heart sounds and measure her jugular venous pressure. Megan appeared, too, as efficient as ever in a suit of black and rust-orange, to hook up an ECG and read the arcane wave patterns that appeared on its screen. She greeted Helen with a friendliness which was rather overdone and, of course, the latter immediately thought, Guilt?

'Yes, look at the right axis deviation.' Megan had turned to Colin Hart.

'Cor pulmonale?' he answered.

'Everything points to it.'

Helen went closer to Mrs Miller and touched the frail old shoulder, saying, 'You'll soon be having some treatment that will make you feel better.'

Mrs Miller frowned faintly then her lids fluttered and she seemed to doze, her nicotine-stained fingers folded over the top of the crisp white sheet.

There was nothing more that Helen could do so she started to leave, but Megan caught up with her at the door. 'You were right to bring her in, Helen. Well done.'

'It was pretty obvious,' Helen answered, finding it a little hard to speak pleasantly. She didn't like this condescending tone of Megan's.

'And apparently you were right about Mrs Kadir, too. It is cotton worker's disease, and Nick will treat it accordingly.'

'Was Mr Kadir relieved at knowing at last? Did he manage to reassure his wife that he won't reject her now? She knows it's not terminal and should actually improve with time, doesn't she?'

'Oh. . .um, I don't know. I only heard the clinical picture, not the personal ramifications.' She laughed rather uncomfortably, and touched a hand to her ash blonde hair in a nervous gesture. 'We've been pretty busy. I just heard that you'd been right in what you suspected, which surprised me because. . .well, frankly, when he told me about it I was sceptical. Oh, my goodness, here he is!'

Her face lit up with a pleasure that would have been quite touching in its innocent openness if the man who'd produced this reaction in her hadn't been Helen's own husband. She herself had her back to the corridor and hadn't seen him, but now she wheeled around, suspicious and miserable—quite certain that she was going to encounter the mirror image of Megan's pleasure in his belovedly familiar face as well. Her stomach was already

dropping and her fists were clenched. She'd never imag-
ined that she would have to live through this—the sight
of Nick's grey eyes lighting up as he looked at another
woman. . .

But his eyes hadn't lit up. He hadn't even looked at
Megan and he was so white and drawn that she lunged
for him, thinking he was ill and convinced that he was
going to faint. 'Nick. . .!'

'Thank God I've found you! I rang the health centre;
I rang Mrs James. Oh, thank God I caught you before
you left again!'

'What is it? What's wrong?' She thought immediately
of the children, of course, and as soon as he held her
and looked into her eyes, her worst fear was confirmed.

'It's Jane. She was in a smash. Pedestrian crossing.
Two cars. On her way out shopping, or something.
They've taken her to Guy's, but she. . . Helen! Helen!
She hasn't regained consciousness yet.'

'Oh. . . Oh. . .' Her legs lost their strength, and she
would have fallen if he hadn't been there, his warmth
and strength and scent the only things she could cling to
to get her through this.

'It happened less than two hours ago. She's stable,
they're saying. Shoulder and femur broken. Some lacer-
ations. And the head injury. They can't tell yet if. . .
if. . .' He took a ragged breath. 'I've got a message out
to Jonathon at the university, but how long before they'll
manage to get it to him. . . We'll take the car. Drive
down at once.' His staccato phrases came between tight
gasps of air, as if his chest were gripped by a
vice-like pain.

'It'll take hours. . .' Helen moaned.

'I know. I know. I thought of flying, or the train, but
by the time we got to the airport or the station—'

'Let's go, then.'

'Megan. . .?' He turned blindly to his senior registrar,

who was white-knuckled as she took in the scene between the two of them.

She said scratchily, 'Yes, Nick, I'll arrange cover, and I'll ring the health centre and get someone to cancel Helen's schedule. Don't worry about anything at this end. Just don't even think about it!' And then, turning wildly to Helen, 'God, I've been such a fool! Can you ever forgive me, Helen? I honestly thought— But I've been living in a fool's paradise, haven't I, all along, and I've made things impossible for you?'

'It doesn't matter now, Megan,' Helen answered, scarcely having heard the emotional words, let alone taken in their meaning.

Megan turned away, her tall figure suddenly awkward and angular and unlovely, and Helen didn't think of her again for some hours.

CHAPTER TEN

NEITHER Helen nor Nick spoke as they left the ward. They didn't need to. There was nothing to say. Even the minute's delay as they waited for the lift to come seemed like an agonising waste of time, and they were both moving almost at a run as they reached Nick's family sedan, parked in the spot reserved for him in the doctors' car park just out the front.

Traffic lights, pedestrian crossings. . . The blood throbbed in Helen's ears like the ticking of a clock.

'What if we don't get there—?' she began, an anguished cry.

But Nick cut her off through clenched teeth. 'Don't say it! Don't! They're saying stable and satisfactory, not critical. She's going to live, Helen.'

'Yes. . . Yes!'

His knuckles were white as he gripped the wheel and yet he drove far more steadily than Helen could have done. She felt a faint, vital trickle of strength returning to her as she sensed him beside her. Whatever happened, she would get through this as long as Nick was there. And he was, now. They were united in this, at least, and she would not, *could* not, think beyond that.

They reached the motorway at last and the speed-ometer needle flirted just above the speed limit, creeping higher until she said, 'Don't. . . Don't, Nick. Go slower.'

'Slower?'

'We need to get there safely. We don't need to get pulled over.'

'No. You're right. I'm sorry. I was just—'

'I know. I know. But we mustn't lose our heads.' She touched his thigh, almost not daring to make the contact, but he took his hand off the wheel for a moment to press his palm against her rigid fingers and so she stayed touching him, feeling the comfort of the gesture almost like an electric current flowing into her.

Three agonising hours later, he asked, 'Do you want to stop and eat?'

'No.'

'No. . .' he agreed.

Not hungry, either of them, although she'd never managed to finish those sandwiches nor her breakfast this morning. Another hour and Nick was pulling into the visitors' car park at Guy's. They were both so disorientated by fatigue and fear that they had to ask for directions twice, until finally a ward clerk going off duty took pity on them and led them to the main desk and on up to the intensive care unit where Jane had been taken.

Nothing seemed to make sense. They were both so familiar with hospitals, and yet this one was just a jarring, jangling blur.

'Mr and Mrs Darnell?' they heard.

'*Dr* Darnell,' Nick managed. 'I'm a consultant thoracic physician at Camberton Hospital, in the north. My wife's a nurse.'

Helen could see that he was holding their professional status out like a magic talisman, as if to say, I'm a doctor—doesn't that qualify us for a miracle?

The nurse nodded kindly. 'Come through, then. You'll know what to expect. She's stable. No change as yet.'

'Right. Yes,' Nick nodded.

Helen couldn't speak. She fell forward to crouch by the high bed, holding back the desperate tears that wanted to come out of some dim realisation that perhaps Jane was aware of them in her coma and mustn't be upset in case it made her condition worse. The hand she held between her own stiffened fingers was her very flesh and blood, Nick's flesh and blood, and it felt so smooth and young and strong that it seemed impossible to believe that Jane wasn't simply asleep. Only this morning, with no premonition of this at all, she had heard Jane's life-filled voice on the phone and now that lovely, precious mouth was silent, opened and slack and already starting to look dry.

Nick was beside her now. 'We're here, Jane,' he said eagerly and tenderly, his voice scratchy and dark with the well of feeling that he was trying to keep at bay. 'We're here now. Had a bit of a hairy trip down, actually. Your mother thought I was speeding, but you know that needle has been dancing up and down the dial for weeks now. I'll have to take it in to get it looked at. I can't possibly have been going at 135 km an hour!'

Helen listened to him in amazement as she rested her shaking arm on the sheet at Jane's side, still holding the limp, fresh young hand. He was talking to her so naturally, using his familiar humour as if she might reply at any moment, and that was right, of course. That was the way to do it—just to talk, to chat, to stimulate that deeply sleeping brain until it woke up.

She couldn't do so. All she wanted to say was, 'Don't die! Don't die! I love you too much to bear it!' and because she knew that it would be wrong to say such heart-rending things she stayed silent, nursing the sour pain inside her, loving Nick's wonderful words and soothed a little by them.

'Rabbit warren of a place, this is!' he went on. 'We got lost twice. I'm sure we went round in circles. . .'

Then there was a noise behind them. 'Mum? Dad?' It was Jonathon.

Helen got to her feet and held her son, his healthy body doubly precious to her now. She put a shaking hand to his untidy dark hair. 'You've just arrived?'

'No, I've been here since four. They tracked me down in a lecture. I just went out for a bit to. . . Well, I tried to eat some chips, but. . .'

He had been crying. Helen could see it in his grey-green eyes now that she looked closely, and the thought that this big, untidy, enthusiastic, gruffly humorous son of hers was still capable of tears brought her own control to the brink again and she couldn't speak; could only nod at his words.

'Mum. . .' he said, and his voice cracked.

'She's going to be all right, Jon,' Helen managed, the mother in her taking over so that she just wanted to shield him from this, and from the reality that Jane might *not* be all right.

'Talk to her, Jon,' Nick said, his voice husky now. 'If she hears your voice perhaps she'll stir.'

'I've tried. I don't know what to say. You know, I'm not very—' He broke off helplessly. He wasn't a talkative type.

'Tell her about your lectures today. Catch her up on gossip—what your friends are doing. Sports news. Anything.'

'Where's Russell?' Helen suddenly blurted. Nick's mention of Jon's and Jane's friends had reminded her. 'Has he been told?'

'I rang him,' Jon said. 'Left a message with someone in his flat. Don't know when he'll get it. But they're not engaged any more. Jane was going to tell you when you came down.'

'Did he break it off?' Helen was hot with fury in a matter of seconds. 'If he did—if he's let her down and isn't here to help and see her through this when for the first time she actually *needs* him. . .!'

'Mum, Mum. . . It's all right.' Jon touched her on the arm with a young man's gruff tenderness. 'They both decided. It's been perfectly friendly, and they still see each other a bit. There's nothing to blame him for.'

'What happened?'

'They just decided it was a bit silly, that's all, and that they'd only done it because they were feeling lonely coming to London.' He added possessively, 'He's always been a bit of a berk, anyway. Jane's worth—'

'She moved!' Nick barked the words, startling Helen and Jonathon and distracting them. But then he pressed a tired, uncertain hand to his temple and rubbed it across his creased eyelids. 'I don't know. I thought. . . Out of the corner of my eye. There's nothing now.'

But Helen had started to lunge towards the bed again. 'Jane? Jane?'

Then wild colour boiled behind her eyes, shading to black, and the room rocked and tilted silently. She felt herself falling and heard the alarmed exclamations of the two male voices she loved best in the world. . .

Nick. Nick was holding her with his strong, safe arms, and she wasn't in Jane's hot, humidified room any more but out near the lifts where there was a small waiting area. Her legs were up on the stretch of vinyl-covered seating and her body was pillowed against his shoulder. It was far cooler here. He was kissing her, kissing her head and her temples, her cheeks and her lips and saying frantically, 'Helen! Darling! Helen. . .'

'It's all right,' she managed fuzzily, and he groaned and held her again—so tightly that she could feel the rapid beat of his pulses. She clung to him as if they were both in danger of drowning and the sobs she had suppressed in Jane's room came jerking out of her, breaking even more strongly when he began to soothe her and stroke her as though she were a child.

And suddenly everything she had been feeling about their marriage over the past month and more came gushing to the surface, and in this crisis that was shaking both of them to their foundations it no longer seemed of the slightest importance to school her words and make them come carefully.

'Nick, don't leave me!' she implored him jerkily. 'I couldn't bear it. I love you so much. I couldn't bear it if our marriage failed. I know it's been hard lately. . . I've been missing the twins, and that's made both of us notice that we'd got a bit staid with each other. I was angry with you, too, for not worrying about Jane's engagement, but now of course I see. . . And it's alienated you, driven you to think that perhaps there's nothing left between us. But I'll do anything I can.

'Tell me what it is that Megan's giving you that I'm not, and if it's in my power. . . Surely you can't love her when. . .when we're both feeling like this about Jane!'

'Megan? Love Megan?' he croaked in amazement. 'My God, have you been thinking—? *How* have you been thinking that? Of course I don't love Megan! Helen, I love *you*, and I thought it was you who thought there was nothing left. . . Yes, the twins going has created a gap, made us both more aware, but I thought it was you who wanted to stay home in England because you cared more about your life here than you did about being with me!'

'Never. . .'

'It's been giving me hell. Then, driving down this afternoon, I suddenly felt close to you again. I knew we were feeling the same—sharing an anguish that no one else could ever share with us in the same way—and that's the *only* thing that got me through those hours in the car. You beside me, touching me. Helen, if you think—!'

'Mum! Dad!' Jonathon burst out of the ward, calling them blindly, his face agitated and alight.

'Here, Jon!' Nick called. Helen leapt to her feet, swayed again and felt his supporting arm at her waist.

'There's been a change. She's stirring and groaning. They think she's coming out of it.'

Helen was speechless and trembling again at once, not willing yet to believe that this was really good news. Her legs would barely carry her back to Jane's room, and it was like wading through thick soup; the yards back into Intensive Care and then to Jane's bedside seemed so long. . .

Her eyes were open. She looked blearily at the three faces of her parents and brother, frowned slightly and closed her lids again, and they heard her voice, thin and weak, 'The blue paramecium. It's sliding. It's off the slide. The blue paramecium.' She lay still again.

'She's not making any sense. She's not making any sense at all!' Jon was almost sobbing. 'Janey! Janey!'

'It's all right, Jon,' Nick said. 'This is quite normal. It's one of the stages of emerging from coma. In fact, she's lightening very fast. Some people take days to get to this point once they first start stirring. But she's been in it a relatively short time. That always gives a good prognosis for full recovery.'

They all watched breathlessly. A nurse entered, unobtrusive and quiet, to check the monitoring equipment. 'She's—'

'Yes,' Nick said. 'Oh, yes! Better every minute.'

Jane's hand was plucking at the sheet now, making the plastic tubing of the IV line taped to her arm coil and uncoil in a snake-like fashion. Her eyes were still closed but her lids were twitching and a moment later her mouth moved as if trying to shape a word, stopped, moved again and she said, 'Camberton?'

'No, darling. . .' Nick bent and touched her arm. 'Guy's Hospital. In London. Remember? You're in London now, studying to be a vet.'

'Of course!' Helen remembered. 'The blue paramecium. She was talking about invertebrates this morning on the phone. Do you remember, Jane? You told me what a lot you knew about them now.'

'No,' Jane said, eyes still closed. Then she opened them. 'Mammal?'

'What, love?'

'I want to say. . .' They all waited. 'Word. Mum. That's right. *Mum.*' Her eyes drifted shut once more.

'Yes, darling-heart, yes, it's me. And Dad, too, and Jon.'

'May I take her observations now?' the nurse asked gently.

'Of course. . .'

'You're doing really well, Jane.' The young Irish woman spoke clearly and cheerfully. 'Can you open your eyes again now? Can you do that? You did it before and I know you can do it again.'

'Can't. . .'

'You can, my lovely. You can, you know.'

'OK. . .' And there they were again—bluer than Nick's, bluer than Jonathon's grey-green, steady and focused now. 'I'm bloody sore!' she said.

An hour later Nick murmured softly, 'She's asleep. We should go, let her rest and come back later tonight.'

'We haven't got anywhere to stay,' Helen said.

'We'll get a hotel room, and I don't care what it costs.'

Jon shifted awkwardly. 'I've got an essay due tomorrow. . .'

'What, and you haven't started it yet?' Nick teased. They all needed his dry humour by this time.

'Haven't *finished* it,' Jon returned indignantly. 'It's at least, oh, a quarter done.'

'Well, you'll be up half the night, then, won't you?'

It was incredible that they could all feel this light-hearted now. Jane's lucid responses so early on had shown that there was no brain damage, and her other injuries, comparatively minor ones, would heal with time. After the black cloud of the past six hours, Helen felt dizzy with joy.

'I will try to get it done, if you don't mind,' Jon was saying earnestly now. For someone outwardly scruffy and casual, he actually took his studies in economics and political science rather seriously. 'It's a good topic. And if I get it in on time I can do some stuff with you lot on the weekend.'

'Get a proper dinner on your way home,' Helen told

him, remembering what he had said about trying and failing to eat some chips earlier.

'Well, I would, only. . .'

Silently, with his mouth tucked in cynically at the corner, Nick handed him a twenty-pound note. Jon grinned. 'Let's see, at the Horse and Coachman this'll get me—' He broke off as Nick made to snatch it back. 'Just a joke, guv, honest!'

'Want a lift?'

'No, I'll get the tube.' He kissed the tips of his fingers and touched them lightly to his twin's forehead, gave a casual salute to his parents and then sloped off.

Helen would have liked to crush him in a fervent, minutes-long embrace, of course, but almost grown-up sons didn't permit this kind of behaviour from their mothers very often, especially when they had already betrayed an unusual degree of emotion that day. She contented herself with a scratchy goodbye and a rough pat on his back instead, then watched him hungrily all the way to the lifts.

'Shall we get going?' Nick said quietly beside her.

'Yes, we must or it'll be horribly late by the time we get settled, and I would like to come back here last thing for a little while, if they'll let us.'

'They will. I checked with the ward sister. Jane will be staying here in the ICU overnight, and they'll move her to the orthopaedic ward tomorrow.'

'All being well. . .'

'All *is* well, Helen,' he assured her, his voice resonant with emotion. 'She's been so lucky.'

Half an hour later they had checked into an outrageously famous and pricey hotel, and Nick said sternly, 'Now, Helen, you must eat!'

'Not a restaurant, though, please!'

'Room service?'

'Perfect!'

He ordered a simple but filling meal by phone, then put down the receiver and turned to her. 'And I have to say I hope it takes a while to arrive.'

'Why, Nick?'

'Because. . .' She was in his arms and his kiss was hungry and tender and inflaming all at once. 'This has been hell. . .'

'Today? Oh, yes! I can't believe it's not even nine, yet.'

'Not just today.' His voice was like a rough caress against her hair. 'These past weeks when I thought— Helen, *why* did you decide you didn't want to go to Boston?'

She broke away and searched his face, amazed. '*I* didn't decide it! It was you! You said, out of the blue when you got back from the conference, that you thought it might be best if I stayed behind. I was so miserable to think that was what you wanted—I was so completely taken by surprise—I couldn't argue back.'

'But you told Megan that you thought it seemed foolish to go, leaving the children at university and the damned *cat*! And the fact that you'd just said that casually to her. . .'

'But I didn't! At least. . .' She searched her memory. 'I *did* say that—about going over for the conference for six days.' Then she recalled, 'And Megan sort of hinted and pushed about it, saying that if it was sensible to stay behind for six days, then surely the same considerations applied over the question of staying or going for a year. I don't think she let me get in a full sentence to insist, that the considerations weren't the same at all, but I never thought she'd report it to you in those terms!'

'She took the interpretation she wanted to take,' Nick growled. 'I only realised today that her funny behaviour lately was the result of a crush. I should have twigged before, I suppose, but I'd always felt. . .rather fatherly towards her and I assumed it was just a matter of professional admiration on her part.'

'I realised how she was feeling just before you went to Boston.'

'Then why on earth didn't you tell me, darling? Tease me about it, or something?'

'I was afraid to,' she admitted, a little ashamed of this. 'I thought it might. . .give you ideas. . .'

'Give me *ideas*?' He was incredulous.

'She's a good doctor, Nick, very bright. . .and *very* beautiful!'

'Beautiful? Rubbish! Well. . .not in the least my type, anyway.'

'What is your type, then?' She dared to be arch.

'Fishing for it?' he laughed. 'Um, chestnut hair, womanly figure. . . No, on second thoughts, I'll tell you later. . .in enormous detail.'

'Mmm, I think I might enjoy that. . .'

'Megan's had a grim home-life, though. In spite of all she has going for her, she has to work through that legacy before she'll make a success of a relationship. One day I'll tell you a bit of what she's told me about her life.'

'Tell me now because, frankly, I'm so angry with her at the moment that I'm finding it difficult to think kindly of her at all, although before all this blew up I felt quite fond of her.'

'Well, alcoholic parents and no support for her ambitions. Could you still be fond of her when you've had time to forgive?' he suggested gently. 'She needs that. . . She's got as far as she has totally on her own will and efforts, and it shows. She thinks that the way to achieve anything—including getting her man—is to go at it like a bull at a gate, ignoring all obstacles. But there's a whole side to her nature that she's ill at ease with, and that's why she's so at sea when it comes to men.'

'She told me straight out that I should step gracefully

aside so that when you were in Boston together you could form a relationship,' Helen said. 'She said it was only your innate decency that was stopping you from having an affair with her now; that you were in love with her but you'd start the process of ending your marriage first, and my staying home from Boston would allow that to happen.'

'And you believed her? My foolish pearl!'

'Because she was so *nice* about it, so nervous and pleading and apparently reasonable. She told me how much she respected and liked me; how adult and civilised she wanted it to be—and she was right about one thing, Nick, you *are* such a decent, honourable man. And I couldn't talk to you about it because I knew I *wouldn't* be reasonable. I'd be a shrieking harridan, totally emotional, and I thought that if there was *any* chance of saving our marriage it could only be my saying nothing about Megan and trying to bridge the distance between us in other ways.

'I found I could believe that you didn't love me any more; that you only stayed with me out of duty because of the struggles we've been through together, and because of the children. It's such a common scenario. And Jon and Jane going did make a hole, more than I've let myself realise, I think. I began to notice things; began to think about how little time we've ever really had to ourselves. For most of our marriage I've had to be a nurse and a mother.'

'And I've felt so guilty sometimes that I didn't insist we wait. You were so young. . .'

'Wait? You couldn't have made me do that. It was all I wanted, and I can't have you feeling guilty about it. But, Nick?'

'Yes, my love?'

'It's. . .not just that, is it? You don't just love me now because I'm the mother of your children?'

'Oh, God, Helen, of course I don't. I love. . . Hell, I

can't even begin to list it all. And if you're really telling me that you don't regret committing your life to me so young. . .'

'Not for a moment,' she whispered.

'Helen. . .' It came out shakily, and he buried his face in her neck and made no further answer in words.

She sought his mouth and gave him her kiss with the same trust and passion that had been in her over twenty years ago when she had given him her virginity, and his touch fanned the slow-burning fire of love within her into white-hot flames of desire that craved satisfaction. He was fully ready to give it. Moments later they were touching skin to skin on the luxurious bed, and they gave themselves to each other with a complete abandon and honesty that had been absent for a long time. . .

Seconds after they finally lay still, a knock sounded at the door.

'Dinner. I'd forgotten all about it. It's taken a while. . . as I hoped! They must have been busy tonight,' Nick said. 'I'll grab a towel. . .'

So Helen stayed dreamily beneath the sheets, watching as he slung the brief rectangle of white cloth casually around his lean hips and daring to believe at last that he was still really hers.

While their meal reposed beneath its insulating covers on the table, she looked for something to put on and realised, saying it aloud, 'We've got no nightclothes.'

He grinned. 'I'm devastated! How can I possibly go to bed beside a woman like you without pyjamas. . .for sheer protection!'

Dressed again, they sat to eat and she noticed for the first time, 'That's champagne in that cooler!'

'Don't you think this is a celebration?'

'For Jane? Oh, yes, and when she's out of hospital we'll have another one.'

'Not just for Jane. A new start for us, Helen.'

'We mustn't be afraid to talk to each other about the things that are important.'

'No, no matter how hard it seems. You'll come to Boston...'

'Try keeping me away!' The pop of the champagne cork punctuated her exclamation.

'I'll have to tell Megan tactfully—Lord knows how— that she's got it all wrong, won't I?' he groaned.

'No, I think she knows now,' Helen answered quietly, remembering the younger woman's telling, emotional phrases to her earlier today. 'She saw how Jane's accident brought us together... I think she knows I'll be coming to Boston.'

'But it does worry me... What will you do? You won't be able to work...'

'I don't want to work,' she told him as they began their soup.

'Then...?'

'I want to do everything else that I haven't done over the past twenty years with you because I always *have* been working.' She sketched it out for him: pursuing some new hobbies; exploring a new city and a new life-style; writing long letters to the twins; planning their visit over the summer; and planning weekends away just for her and Nick; cooking special meals. 'That's if you could stand to have me fussing over you.'

'I think I could...just!'

'I feel I've never been able to, and you've worked so hard—you've deserved so much more than my sketchy cooking and cleaning.'

'There are other considerations, though.'

'*Not* Pushcart?'

'Not Pushcart! But the house.'

'Sell it?' she pleaded tentatively.

'Sell it?'

'It's so darned *practical*, Nick. I don't want us to be practical any more. I want to rent an elegant high-ceilinged apartment in Boston and then, when we come back. . .'

'It could be as long as three years.'

'All the better! I want us to buy a thatched cottage, or a turreted mansion, or an old mill like Liz and Pete.'

'I do like their mill. Shall we drop in on them on our way home, Sunday afternoon?'

'I'd rather do a preliminary scout on our china.'

'Acquisitive creature!'

'I hate the fact that we've had to put it off.'

'So do I,' he admitted. 'We never give ourselves decent presents! Our china wedding anniversary after all. . .'

'And, Nick. . .?' Since she was being totally honest tonight—at last daring to believe that it was safe and right to do so—and since he himself had just said how important it was that they talk about the things that mattered. . .

'Yes?' His eyes, in the lights she had carefully dimmed, looked dark and deep and glowing, and in his maturely handsome face she saw all the boyishness she'd loved in him for twenty years.

She was scared to say it, but she pressed on. To say nothing, she now knew, would be far worse. 'After another year or so, if you could bear it, if you wanted it too, I. . .I'd like to start having another baby.' She held her breath, prepared for the worst. If he didn't want to, then she could accept it. She would have to think instead about—

But his whole face was alive with a laughing pleasure, and there was no ambivalence whatsoever in his expression or his words. 'Oh, darling, *would* you?' he said. 'Would you really?'

'I'd like nothing better in the whole world,' she whispered.

Later that night, after another visit to Jane, Nick suggested very earnestly that they ought to practise the mechanics of it a bit if they could manage it at this late hour. 'After all, we're not as young as we once were. Do you think I've still got what it takes?'

'I'm not too worried about it,' she assured him kindly. 'But by all means let's practise if you want to. You could be right. No sense in getting rusty. We'll probably have to train intensively for the event for months before we finally put the plan into action.'

'I think I'm going to enjoy these next few years,' Nick murmured against her mouth.

'Every minute, my love,' she whispered in reply.

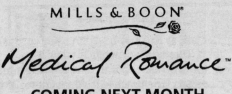

MILLS & BOON®

Medical Romance™

COMING NEXT MONTH

A GIFT FOR HEALING by Lilian Darcy
Camberton Hospital

Karen Graham's manipulative ex-boyfriend, who was sick
with TB, wanted her back. Guilt-ridden, she had no-one to
turn to except Lee Shadwell. He was more than willing to
offer friendship and support. Karen knew she was loved and
in love, but with which man?

POWERS OF PERSUASION by Laura MacDonald

Nadine vowed to remain immune to the charms of the new
Italian registrar Dr Angelo Fabrielli. But that proved
impossible when he moved into her house—and her heart!
But she refused to be his wife knowing that she could never
give him the one thing he needed most...

FAMILY TIES by Joanna Neil

The new locum, Dr Matthew Kingston, was critical and a
touch too arrogant so Becky Laurens kept her distance.
But that proved difficult when she found him incredibly
attractive. Becky had to end things with her current
boyfriend—but was Matthew willing to take his place?

WINGS OF CARE by Meredith Webber
Flying Doctors

Radio operator, Katy Woods, was secretly in love with
Dr Peter Flint. So when he was trapped during a cyclone
she willingly offered words of comfort. And on his return
Peter made it clear that he wanted Katie! But did he
want commitment?

FREE!

FOUR FREE
specially selected
Medical Romance™ novels
PLUS a FREE Mystery Gift
when you return this page...

Return this coupon and we'll send you 4 Medical Romance novels and a mystery gift absolutely FREE! We'll even pay the postage and packing for you.

We're making you this offer to introduce you to the benefits of the Reader Service™– FREE home delivery of brand-new Medical Romance novels, at least a month before they are available in the shops, FREE gifts and a monthly Newsletter packed with information, competitions, author profiles and lots more...

Accepting these FREE books and gift places you under no obligation to buy, you may cancel at any time, even after receiving just your free shipment. Simply complete the coupon below and send it to:

MILLS & BOON READER SERVICE, FREEPOST, CROYDON, SURREY, CR9 3WZ.

READERS IN EIRE PLEASE SEND COUPON TO PO BOX 4546, DUBLIN 24

NO STAMP NEEDED

Yes, please send me 4 free Medical Romance novels and a mystery gift. I understand that unless you hear from me, I will receive 4 superb new titles every month for just £2.20* each, postage and packing free. I am under no obligation to purchase any books and I may cancel or suspend my subscription at any time, but the free books and gift will be mine to keep in any case. (I am over 18 years of age)

M7XE

Ms/Mrs/Miss/Mr_____
BLOCK CAPS PLEASE

Address_____

_____

_____ Postcode _____